LOVE

AT

LAST

DOROTHY EWELS

ISBN: 978-0-6399631-2-9 (Ebook: Mobi)
ISBN: 978-0-6399631-3-6 (Paperback)

Any references to historical events, real people, or real places are used fictitiously. Names, characters, and places are products of the author's imagination. Any resemblance to actual events or locales or persons, living or dead, is entirely coincidental.

Front cover design: Raven Designs.
Formatting by Raven Designs.
Edited by Candice Royer
Proofread by Illuminate Author Services

First edition 2019.

www.dorothyewels.co.za

To the man who is the wings that permit me to fly. Thank you for

encouraging me to soar, no matter how scary the flight.

Thank you for being my safety net. I love you.

CHAPTER ONE

The moment she closed the door behind her, Willow realised something was wrong. Silence permeated the house, and the unexpectedness of it unsettled her. Since her friend, Meri, had moved in with her two months ago, the house was never quiet anymore. Meri loved music and always had it playing in some part of the house. Tonight though — nothing. Maybe she was overreacting, and Meri had just gone out. She really hoped that was the case.

"Meri? Are you home?"

More silence.

Willow moved farther into the house looking to see if she could find a note explaining the quiet; the lack of response. It was unlike Meri to go out without leaving a note or not to have told her in advance.

"Meri?" she called again as she moved into the living room. "Are you here, babes?"

Nothing.

"Meri, are you home?" she called once more, unease crawling its way along her spine.

Shrugging out of her jacket, she walked back to the hallway to hang it up. A low, pain-filled moan caught her attention. The uneasiness ramped up. Moving through the hallway, she called once more, "Meri, are you in here? Are you okay, babes?"

Willow stopped to listen, trying to pinpoint exactly where the sound was coming from, hoping to hear it again so it would point her in the right direction. Then she heard the moan anew. Realising it was coming from the living room, she moved toward it. As she rounded the long sofa, she stopped in her tracks, unable to comprehend the sight before her. Meri lay on the ground, curled up on her side in a fetal position, clearly trying to protect the twins she was heavily pregnant with. She was severely beaten, lying in an ever-growing pool of blood beneath her hip. Icy panic flashed through Willow. That amount of blood couldn't mean anything good for Meri's pregnancy.

"Oh God, Meri." Willow dropped to her knees beside her friend. "Babes, can you hear me? Meri? Meri!"

Getting no response, Willow jumped to her feet. She raced back to the hallway to get her cell phone. Her hands shook so badly she misdialled three times before she finally managed to get through to the cell phone emergency line — 112.

"One-one-two, what is your emergency, please?"

Giving her name, Willow told the operator what the problem was as quickly and concisely as she could.

As the tears coursed down her face and her breath hitched, Willow could barely manage a whisper. "Please. She's pregnant, and . . . Oh God, there's just so much blood."

"Stay with me here, Ms Martin. I've dispatched an ambulance and the police. They're on their way to you as we speak," the operator soothed.

While staying on the line, Willow kept talking to Meri, trying to get her to respond. It seemed to Willow as if the blood was rapidly expanding. She was so far out of her depth that panic, icy and insidious, held her in a tight grip. By the time emergency services and police arrived, Willow's panic was full-fledged. She had never felt so alone in her life.

Standing to one side, so she was out of the way, she watched everything the paramedics did as they worked on her friend.

Just when Adam thought the day couldn't get crappier, it finally ended. He couldn't get away from the station quickly enough. He felt called to be a policeman since he was a little boy. It was all he remembered ever wanting to be. But days like today made him question the wisdom of his choice. Crime, in general, offended his moral code, but when it involved children, as today's case had, it was always difficult to deal with. It cut especially close to the bone now that he had a child of his own.

Giving thanks that he'd at least get to hold his infant daughter again, he headed to collect her from her day mother. He looked forward to some downtime to decompress, maybe relaxing on the couch with a cold one after he'd gotten Gracie settled for the night. A couple of blocks from home, his cell phone rang, interrupting the sounds of rock music flowing through the stereo as his daughter slept on in her car seat.

His partner ringing at this time of evening generally wasn't a good sign. It would seem likely that his crappy workday wasn't quite over yet. Biting back a sigh, he answered.

"Hey, Gav. What's up, bud?"

"Hey, man. Just got a call in from dispatch. One-one-two caught an assault, possibly attempted murder. I caught the case, but since I'm headed off on sick leave for my shoulder op in a couple days, Cap's decided he wants you to take over from me as the lead on this one. I'm almost at the scene now. I'll message you the address as soon as I get there. You can meet me there."

Mentally cursing, using every imaginative expletive he knew, Adam turned the car around, heading towards his parents' house instead of his own.

"Let me just drop Gracie off at my mom's. I'll be there as soon as I can."

He disconnected the call, dialled his mom, and ten minutes later dropped his sleeping baby off with his parents.

"Thanks, Mom. I appreciate it." Bending, Adam placed a gentle kiss on the older woman's cheek.

"You're welcome, my boy. Don't worry about Gracie. We'll keep her here tonight. Dad and I can drop her off at daycare in the morning. You just head straight home when you're done. A good night's rest will do you good. You're looking tired, my boy. You work too hard."

He thanked his mother again. After giving his daughter one last kiss on the head and hugging his mother goodbye, he headed to the address his partner had messaged him.

Pulling up to the house on a quiet street in an ordinarily tranquil neighbourhood, Adam absently noted the flashing lights. A few people stood around watching the commotion, huddling together and murmuring amongst themselves. It certainly was a sight out of the ordinary for them. Approaching the front door, he found it standing wide open, vehicles and people stood all over the driveway.

He stepped into the foyer and looked around for his partner. When he didn't spot Gavin, he called a uniformed officer over to inquire as to where to find him. She informed him the man was in the living room, pointing him in the right direction.

As he moved that way, he caught the sound of quiet weeping. Clearly distraught, they obviously needed someone with a gentle touch dealing with them tonight, but after the miserable day he'd had, it couldn't be him. He was all out. As he turned back to find the uniform he'd just spoken with, he caught a glimpse of a beautiful woman talking to a paramedic. He took a step closer to get a better look and felt somewhat dazed – a bit like he'd walked into a brick wall.

She was a tiny bundle of perfect. The policeman in him was ingrained. Even when admiring a good-looking woman, his well-trained eye assessed. He estimated she couldn't be more than five foot two or three. Although not overweight, she certainly had the voluptuous curves that a man craved to get his hands on. A mass of blonde waves tumbled down her back to just below her waist.

Pulling his gaze away from her, he started turning away. In his current mood, it was probably best to leave her to Gavin. He was good with people. He'd know what to say to make her feel at ease.

She chose that moment to unexpectedly turn her head, looking directly at him.

His heart clenched at the sight of her tear-drenched eyes, the colour of the deepest blue sapphires, still so beautiful despite the tears. Suddenly, he had an intense desire to haul her into his arms and comfort her, which made no sense at all.Adam had never had such a visceral reaction to anyone before. Changing his mind, Adam moved towards her. Those intense blue eyes followed his progress as he crossed the floor.

A sense of being watched penetrated the fog in Willow's brain. She turned her head to seek out the source and spotted a man standing in the doorway of her living room. Although she immediately noticed he was handsome, despite her grief, it was more than that. He had a presence about him that commanded attention. Their eyes met, and her brain seemed to stall. For a long moment, she seemed incapable of speech. She simply stared. And in that long moment, the horror of her surroundings retreated from her thoughts.

"My apologies for intruding at a difficult time, ma'am. I'm detective Adam Dawson – the investigating officer in this case. I just need to ask you a few questions."

"I'm not sure how much I can help you. I didn't see anything. I found her like this."

"No problem, ma'am." Adam smiled reassuringly. "Let's see what we can piece together, okay?"

Nodding hesitantly, Willow agreed.

"What is the victim's name?"

"Merida Davids."

"And what's your relationship to Ms Davids, ma'am?"

"She's my friend. She recently got out of a relationship and has been staying with me while she gets back on her feet."

Looking back over at Meri, she closed her eyes against a sharp pain in the region of her heart. Willow tried to breathe through the pain and panic. She couldn't envisage a life without Meri in it.

They'd been friends since nursery school. Their

friendship had endured school, boyfriends, university, the craziness of youth – queuing for hours in the pouring rain for concert tickets, an urge to drink shots at three in the morning while belting show tunes at the top of their lungs. She couldn't remember a time they hadn't been there for each other. It had even survived Meri's relationship with a man whose solution to everything was violence. Thankfully, it seemed JJ had finally managed to destroy their relationship beyond repair with his wild jealousy and violent temper.

"Was there a particular reason she left the relationship, Ms Martin? Or was it a case of it having run its course?" the detective asked.

"Her partner was abusive. He was always good at using his fists. If he had a point to make, a beating was his way of getting it across." Willow saw no need to beat around the bush.

She'd always feared one day his violent temper

would result in one of those beatings being the death of Meri. But eventually, Meri came to her senses, leaving him when the last beating resulted in yet another hospital visit. When she discovered she was pregnant with JJ's twins, she'd voiced fears that if she didn't leave, it could very well end in tragedy. So, she'd packed her bags and moved in with Willow.

Willow was worried about Meri though. She loved having Meri living with her, but it hurt to watch her friend slip deeper and deeper into depression as time passed. Clearly, Meri missed JJ, but he was toxic for her.

"Do you have any idea when last Ms Davids had any contact with her ex-partner?"

"I'm not sure exactly, but I do know that since she moved in, he's been coming around to the house and phoning her constantly, begging her to come home."

It had concerned Willow. She could see JJ's constant presence was eroding Meri's hard-won resolve not to go back to him.

"When was the last time you saw Ms Davids?"

"We had breakfast together this morning before I left for work at around eight thirty. She wanted to know what she should make for dinner, as usual. Meri decided when she moved in that she would take care of the household duties while she stayed, as her way of making a contribution." Willow's voice hitched. "That was the last time I saw or spoke to her."

Tears trailed down her face as the realisation dawned that it might very well be the last thing she and Meri got to talk about ever again. She was very grateful to the big detective for giving her a moment when he handed her a handkerchief from his jacket pocket and said nothing more.

A sound behind her had that hypnotic gaze swinging away from him, effectively releasing him. His gaze shifting beyond her. He noticed the paramedics moving toward him.

As they wheeled the gurney past him, he a saw a young woman lying there. Nasty bruising was already visible, but underneath the vivid colouring, her skin was deathly pale. What snagged his attention was the enormous baby bump starkly highlighted by the white sheet covering her. It seemed today was his day for all the lousy cases. Stepping aside, he let the paramedics through on their way out to the ambulance.

Forensics passed the gurney at the front door. The same police officer who'd assisted Adam pointed them towards the living room, and they moved towards where he stood. The room behind him was in complete disarray, bearing testament to the fact that the victim on the gurney had clearly put up one hell of a fight. Sadly, it didn't seem as if it had done her any good. He knew the best way he could help this poor woman was to find out who had done this and bring them to justice.

The metallic sound of the gurney being locked into place snagged her attention. She saw the paramedics wheeling Meri towards the door. Turning back to the detective, Willow spoke again.

"Forgive me, detective, I have to go with Meri now. I'm all she has left. I'll arrange with my neighbour, Ms Ellis, to come over. She'll lock up behind you."

"I understand, ma'am. It's no problem. I'll be in touch to follow up a little later then."

Thanking him, she headed for the foyer. As she collected the jacket she'd hung there what seemed like forever ago now, she made a quick call to her elderly neighbour to ask her to come over. Someone needed to be there while the police processed the crime scene – her home. She needed to be with Meri.

Ms Ellis, always so willing to help, promised to be right over.

Spotting the elderly lady coming up the drive

as she reversed her car out, Willow stopped but left it idling as she got out to speak to her neighbour. With a hug and a heartfelt thank you, she climbed back into her car to follow the ambulance to the hospital. Beside herself with fear for her friend, Willow cried the entire drive to the hospital.

CHAPTER TWO

In the short time, she'd been standing at Meri's bedside in the intensive care unit, Willow had come to despise the antiseptic smell and the mechanical sounds of the life support machines keeping her friend tethered to life. She hadn't thought they would let her stay the night with Meri as they weren't blood-related. But since she was pretty much all her friend had left in life, they allowed her in, feeling that her familiar presence would be soothing to the other woman.

Her heart ached as she looked down at the hideously injured woman lying in bed before her. Tears welled, yet again, streaking down her reddened cheeks. She'd cried so many tears already since she found her best friend lying on her living room floor, she thought there were no more left. Apparently, she was wrong.

She reached out and took Meri's hand in hers. It was icy cold. She lifted it to her cheek, cradling it gently as she tried to warm it. Through the tears, she looked down, silently willing Meri to open her eyes. She felt lost, adrift without her vibrant presence. There was never a dull moment when they were together. She would give almost anything to have Meri wake up. To see that enchanting smile of hers that always lit up the room and drew people to her.

A quiet clearing of a throat caused Willow to whip around. Standing behind her was the handsome man from the previous night. Not sure why she hadn't expected him to show up so soon, she stared at him blankly for a moment. So much had happened since then, she hadn't given him another thought.

She was surprised she hadn't; he was most definitely memorable.

He had a handsome face saved from being beautiful by a rather nasty scar running from just in front of his left ear, curling around the bottom part of his cheek and disappearing under his chin. In a distant part of her mind, she wondered how badly it had hurt.

A strong, square jaw gave him a rather formidable appearance, but he had surprisingly full, soft-looking lips that went a long way to soften his face when he smiled. Intelligent eyes the colour of polished amber looked out from under straight eyebrows. And those eyes were focused squarely on her. Despite the dire circumstances, she couldn't help but feel a flutter of awareness in her stomach.

"I hope I'm not intruding?" the man enquired.

Giving him another once over, Willow tried to marshal her thoughts.

"No, it's fine," she finally answered. "I remember seeing you at the house last night. Do you have news?"

Willow watched in fascination as those lips quirked up in a brief smile.

"Apologies, ma'am. I don't. I have more questions, and I need to take down a written statement from you."

The detective, Adam, she recalled belatedly stuck his hand out in greeting. Willow hesitated a moment but took it eventually. She stilled as electricity raced up her arm. Pulling her tingling hand away from his, she returned his smile with an uncertain one of her own.

"What more can I tell you?"

"Ms Martin, there are a couple of points you spoke about last night I'd like to follow up on. I was wondering if you perhaps have some time now?"

"To be honest, like I mentioned last night, I really don't know much. I'm not sure how I can be of any further help. As I said, that's how I found her when I got home. It won't surprise me if JJ is involved in this though. This is exactly his style."

"I'm interested in a bit of background regarding Ms Davids. There might very well be something there that will point this investigation in the right direction. Based on how well you know Ms Davids."

"Yes, Meri and I have been best friends since we were about five."

"Could I steal you away for a few minutes? Maybe chat at the coffee shop? That way if you're needed, they can call you, and you'll be able to get back here quickly." At her nod of assent, Adam gestured for her to precede him from the room to the elevators.

Willow took a seat at a table while Adam went to get their coffee at the counter. She took the time to study him, again marvelling at how comfortable she felt in his company despite not knowing him at all. Not having much exposure to male company growing up, she wasn't usually at ease being around men other than her brother. At least not until she got to know them. He just seemed to give off "trust me" vibes.

Adam returned to the table with their coffee, cutting her reverie short. Sitting down opposite her, he took a notebook and pen from the inside pocket of his sports jacket. Willow found herself surprised at how much information he'd already gathered. Clearly, he'd been busy since last night. The questions were astute and well-honed, digging for maximum knowledge to get a sharply accurate picture.

Willow wasn't sure if it was the stress of the last twenty-four hours, or that she felt at ease with the detective, but she found the words just tumbling out, sharing with him all the things that had plagued her about JJ all these years. She shared about his violent temper and all the times it had led to Meri being rushed to the hospital. How it had always been her greatest fear that one of the beatings JJ gave Meri would eventually lead to her friend's demise. She even told him of her suspicions – that despite a lack of evidence, she was convinced that JJ was the person responsible for this one too.

Eventually, Willow's outburst wound down. For a moment, she felt embarrassed to have ranted like that. But she also felt lighter for having finally gotten all of it off her chest. They were nearly done, with just a couple more questions to go, when Willow's cell phone rang, and she recognised the hospital's number.

"Oh God, Meri!" was all she said as she whirled out of her chair and sprinted for the stairs, in too much of a rush to wait for the elevator.

Adam followed her quickly, skidding to a halt at the nurses' station to see Willow huddled over to the side, staying well out of the way as the staff worked on reviving her friend. The machines Meri was attached to beeped, hissed, and jangled as they worked valiantly and fought desperately to keep her alive.

Willow was ashen and her eyes enormous as she stared at the chaos before her. The pain and horror etched on her beautiful face had him clenching his hands in impotent fury. He had no way to change what had been done and no way to comfort her in the face of a rather inevitable outcome. Nobody was saying it, but he'd borne witness to too many scenes like this one to believe there'd be a happy ending to this regretable story.

Suddenly, the group around the bed parted as the nurse at the head began to wheel the bed towards the door. Another nurse went over to speak to Willow. As the other nurses rushed past him, he heard the words "operating theatre three, premature labour, and haemorrhaging" uttered. Looking back over, he saw the nurse holding Willow's hand, still talking to her. As if the news the nurse was sharing with her was a burden too heavy to bear, Willow sank to the floor sobbing like her heart was breaking.

Walking over to the nurse, he indicated he'd take it from there. Grateful, she gave him a sad, tired smile and left them to it. He sank down beside Willow on the floor. After a brief internal battle, he placed an awkward arm around Willow's shoulders. They sat like that until she finally cried herself out. Then they sat in silence as they waited for news.

CHAPTER THREE

The memorial service over, Willow made her way out of the beautiful little chapel in the picturesque coastal village of St James, Cape Town. She took a moment to appreciate the exquisite view of False Bay as she gathered her composure. She wasn't sure she was ready to face any one of a handful of people who had come to pay their respects to Meri. Grief cut sharp and deep.

Willow felt as if there was an enormous weight lying on her chest. She couldn't seem to draw an easy breath. Still reeling from the loss of her friend, she couldn't seem to find peace of mind either. Meri's twin girls were currently under protection in the neonatal ICU as law enforcement waited to hear from authorities what was to be the fate of babies'. Willow was hoping that the other woman had made provisions for her children.

Making her way down the church path to the parking lot, she noticed a dark-haired man leaning against her car. He faced away from her, apparently enjoying the same view she'd been admiring. In the moment it took to realise it was Adam Dawson, she'd gone ice cold. For that very brief moment, she'd thought JJ was waiting for her. He'd been leaving her random messages and making threatening phone calls late at night. During the first call he'd made, he'd gone so far as to blame her for Meri's death. He'd managed to twist it in his mind, so no blame lay at his own door.

In all the years Willow had known JJ, he'd never taken responsibility for his actions. It was always someone else's fault that he behaved the way he did.

Therefore, he felt entirely justified in lashing out at her, threatening her.

Coming to a stop in front of Adam, once more she tried to gather herself. She felt emotional, raw after all that had happened in the last two weeks. And later that day, she'd be going to the attorney's office to hear Meri's last wishes. She didn't feel ready. It made it all too final. But she was the only one who could do it. It fell to her to make sure her lifelong friend's behests would be carried out.

Other than the fact that her friend had wanted to be cremated, Meri had never actually shared with her what she wanted for her children should anything happen to her. No doubt Willow would be finding out soon enough.

She avoided Adam's gaze as he assessed her with the eyes of a seasoned policeman, eyes that missed nothing. An awkward silence ensued since neither could find the right words to break it. Willow wasn't even sure how he'd managed to find her in the first place. Eventually, she broke the silence.

"Good morning, Detective. This is a surprise."

"Ms Martin. I was wondering if you had a spare moment or two?"

Unsure how to read the tone of his voice, Willow took a moment before she answered, weighing her words before responding.

"Now isn't a good time. I have an appointment in a short while. Is it something that can wait?"

Straightening away from her vehicle, Adam nodded.

"Yes, of course. Sure thing. Give me a call when you're free."

Instead of walking away, as she'd expected him to do, Adam once again gave her a measured look. He looked like he wanted to say something but wasn't sure how. After a long, uncomfortable moment, he spoke again.

"Are you doing okay? You look like you're not getting any rest."

A rather expressive eyebrow rose gracefully, a small smile tilting her lips.

"Is that your polite way of telling me I look like hell, Detective?"

A dull red crept into Adam's cheeks, and he had the grace to look sheepish.

"Sorry. That didn't come out right. You look beautiful. I just meant you – um – never mind. I should probably let you get going. Don't want you to be late for your appointment."

He looked so aghast at the words coming out of his mouth that for the first time in what seemed like forever Willow found herself laughing. She couldn't help it. It felt rusty but so good.

"Relax, Detective, I'm just teasing. I know you meant well. But you're right, I need to get going. I'll give you a call as soon as I have a minute."

Willow pressed her car's remote to unlock her door. Before she could open it though, Adam stepped around her and opened it for her.

"Thank you."

Nodding, he replied, "Drive carefully," before turning and walking away.

Puzzled by the odd exchange, she sat and stared at the retreating figure for a moment before starting her car. She didn't want to be late.

Lame, Dawson. Lame! Could you possibly have embarrassed yourself any more? Adam derided himself as he made his way back to his own vehicle. He still had no idea what had possessed him to follow her all the way out to the southern suburbs of Cape Town, miles away from his northern suburb office. But he'd known that it was her friend's memorial service today and had felt a strong urge to be there for her. This was so out of character for him.

Something about this woman drew him to her. On the surface, she gave the impression of being a strong woman, but he also got the impression there was a fragile interior hidden deep within. So, he'd gone to the memorial service. Maybe he was crazy, but he wanted to make sure she was okay. He stayed out of sight, sitting at the back of the church. But just being there soothed something in him, knowing that if she needed a shoulder to lean on, he would be on hand to offer one.

He'd wanted to go over and comfort her when she'd broken down during the service. It had taken willpower not to. Watching her cry had been difficult. Something he thought he was long immune to. His ex-wife had used tears as a tool to manipulate – people and situations – to her will. He'd finally wised up and grown indifferent. She'd taken to calling him cold-hearted when it stopped working. But Willow

Martin's tears had been a genuine expression of how deep the hurt ran. And it had made him want to soothe the pain.

Get a grip, dude! This is an active investigation. Just where exactly do you think this thing could go anyway? She's off limits. Adam dropped his forehead to the roof of his car in disgust. What the hell was wrong with him? Where was the professionalism he prided himself on? As the complainant in her friend's murder, Willow Martin was out of his reach. If his captain got an inkling that he had these thoughts, he'd take him off the case fast enough to give him whiplash.

If he wanted to help her find justice for her friend, he was going to have to put thoughts of Willow out of his mind. When he saw her pull out of the parking lot, he climbed into his own car and drove the forty minutes back to his office. He had a ton of work to do, and none of it included mooning over the gorgeous Ms Martin.

The offices of Fitzsimmons and Reed were elegant and understated. Willow was greeted by the receptionist who whisked her off to a private waiting area away from the hustle and bustle of the open reception room. Having barely waited five minutes, she'd been collected by the attorney's personal assistant and escorted to the office of Patrick Fitzsimmons.

"Good day, Ms Martin. Please have a seat."

Murmuring a greeting, Willow took a seat in front of the large oak desk at which he sat.

"Before we start, I would like to extend my condolences. Ms Davids was such a lovely young lady. I was sorry to hear of her passing."

Swallowing down the lump in her throat at his words, Willow replied, "Thank you, Mr Fitzsimmons. It's been a difficult couple of weeks."

"I can imagine." Pausing, he gave her a moment to compose herself before continuing. "Well, let's get down to the business of why you're here."

She simply nodded.

"I have known Merida since she was a little girl. Her grandmother was originally my client, and when she passed, she left everything to her granddaughter. I was entrusted with looking after Merida's affairs. A couple of years ago, she came to me fearing for her life and asked that I draw up a comprehensive, ironclad will should anything happen to her. Sadly, it seems, she was right to be concerned."

Emotion crossed the older gentleman's face, and Willow realised he'd been quite fond of Meri. She shouldn't be surprised; Meri had always had that effect on people.

"What I find so difficult to accept is that she'd left that situation. She'd been staying with me while trying to get back on her feet."

"No, my dear. Merida was staying with you because she needed *you*, not because she needed to get back on her feet. She was a rather wealthy young lady."

Reeling in shock, Willow simply stared at the man. She didn't know what to say. How had she and Meri been such close friends from childhood, yet Meri had never shared something so personal with her?

"I'm sorry, my dear. I can see this comes as quite a shock. Merida only learned of her inheritance when she turned twenty-one. She didn't want it to change her life or the way people saw her. She'd seen the change in her parents before their passing, and she didn't want the same thing happening in her life."

Needing a moment to gather herself, Willow went over to the window and stared out sightlessly. Her jumbled thoughts were focused inward. Her heart ached that her friend had felt she couldn't share her good news. But as the shock wore off and she thought about it more, it made sense. JJ was possessive enough as it was. She could only imagine how much worse it would have gotten if he'd known. He would probably have felt entitled to a share of the money. She was sure he'd have found some twisted way to justify it in his mind. Taking a deep breath to settle herself, she returned to her seat.

"I'm sorry. That was a bit of a jolt. I just needed a moment. Please, continue."

Giving Willow a kindly smile, the attorney went on.

"Merida has divided her estate equally between you and her two infant daughters. You'll each receive a third. In your case, the money will be transferred to you as soon as everything is settled. In the case of the twins, theirs will go into a trust I am in the process of setting up for them until they're twenty-one."

Mr Fitzsimmons continued to lay out the terms

and conditions of the last will and testament of Merida Elizabeth Davids as finalised just a scant three months earlier. It seemed as if Meri had intuitively known she was running out of time. When he finally got around to mentioning what exactly her third entailed, Willow felt her jaw drop open but seemed incapable of remedying the situation. The bombshell had her reeling yet again.

"Surely there must be some mistake?" she finally managed.

"No, my dear. There's no mistake."

"Are you sure?" Shaking her head, Willow held up a hand. "Of course, you're sure."

Smiling, the older gentleman nodded.

"Mr Fitzsimmons, what about Chelsea and Kelly? Did Meri make any provision for the girls other than financially?" she continued.

"Ah yes, the twins' custody. According to her wishes, she requested that the High Court be petitioned to appoint you as their legal guardian, should you be willing to accept such responsibility."

"Absolutely. Yes. Absolutely! How soon would we be able to start proceedings? How long would it take before I can bring the girls home?"

Laughing, Mr Fitzsimmons replied, "It warms my heart to see you so eager, Ms Martin. Now that we've ascertained you're willing, we'll get the ball rolling. The court rolls are quite full, but we'll see what we can do to get the matter expedited so we can get those little ones into your home and care as soon as possible. I know a few people. I'll see what favours I can call in."

Willow filled in the paperwork required of her, and the meeting wrapped up not too much later. Getting to his feet, Mr Fitzsimmons held out his hand to Willow. Willow took it.

"It's been a pleasure, Ms Martin. Well, as far as it can be under the circumstances, anyway."

"Thank you, Mr Fitzsimmons. For everything." As emotions rose up again, Willow tried to wipe a lone tear away as surreptitiously as possible. A bit awkwardly, Mr Fitzsimmons patted a fatherly hand on her back in silent understanding.

"My pleasure, young lady. I'll be in touch as soon as I have news for you."

Letting go of her hand, the older gentleman escorted her to the door, opening it for her when they reached it. Bidding him a final farewell, Willow made her way down to her car in a daze from all the news she'd just received.

Better than most, Willow knew they all had their own demons to slay. Climbing into her car, Willow rested her head against the steering wheel. The emotions of the day crashed over her, and she had to take a moment to catch her breath. Closing her eyes, Willow vowed to Meri that she would love her children and raise them as if they were her own, giving them the best life she could.

CHAPTER FOUR

Amid the happy laughter and the sound of little feet running over the flagstone in joyful abandon, Willow stood and watched her daughters playing in the bright African sunlight.

Absently, she rubbed a hand over her heart. She'd never bought into the concept that romance novels had glamorised about heartache being a physical thing, but in that moment, as she watched the children running around hyped on sugar and high on the excitement of life, she came to the realisation that heartache could, indeed, be a very physical pain.

For the most part, the past four years had been difficult. The shock of losing Meri had been like losing a vital part of herself. But the blessing of having her friend's babies in her life had helped her to keep it together in order to bring up these two gorgeous little lives she'd left behind. Since Meri had been the last surviving member of her family, and she hadn't wanted JJ anywhere near the children, she'd made it a stipulation in her will that an application be made to the High Court that Willow be appointed as their guardian.

Today, they were celebrating the twins' fourth birthday. It was both a blessing and a sorrow. A blessing that she'd gotten to spend the last four years with these two bundles of joy and energy, heart-breaking that she'd had to do it without Meri.

These two precious children had meant everything to her friend. Meri's dream had been to have a happy family with JJ. She'd clung to that dream until it had killed her. Quite literally. While she'd been dreaming of domestic bliss, he'd been perpetrating domestic violence, and she paid for that dream with her life.

Pulling herself from her distressing thoughts, she heard little voices chanting.

"Mommy, mommy, mommy. Is it time to cut the cake yet?"

Laughing down into the excited faces of her little girls, she could only nod as she swallowed around the knot still firmly lodged in her throat.

"Come on, you two little rascals. Let's go get some yummy cake."

The sound of the doorbell added to the general mayhem. Turning to one of her school mom friends, she asked her to just keep an eye on the little ones while she went to answer the door. She wondered who it might be since it was a bit early for the parents to be collecting their children already.

Momentarily, a sense of dread washed through

her as she reached for the handle. At the most random moments, she feared JJ would resurface, as he'd been threatening to do since he caused Meri's death. Even though the last beating he gave Meri had led to her death, he blamed Willow for everything, the failure of his relationship with Meri, her death, that Willow had guardianship of the twins, and that the police wanted to question him regarding Meri's death. It seemed to be well beyond his realm of self-awareness to grasp that he had no one to blame but himself.

Opening the door, Willow was greeted by a face that was almost instantly familiar. A face that intensified the sick feeling of dread already coursing through her. She hadn't seen him in nearly three years since the investigation had run cold. For a moment, it hurt to look at him as the memories swamped her. How bizarre that today of all days, when she was already struggling with overwhelming sadness, he would show up on her doorstep.

He took a step back and gave her an equally startled look. Taking another step back he then gave the house a quick once-over before turning back to her. Silence stretched between them before he spoke in that husky voice that conjured up thoughts of hot, sweaty nights and satin sheets. All he said was, "Willow Martin."

Blinking, Willow wasn't quite sure how to respond, her thoughts scrambled. Why was he here? It had been just less than three years since the trail had run cold and Meri's murder had become yet another cold case, filed away in a dusty archive somewhere. JJ had successfully managed to evade prosecution since there was no evidence tying him to the murder of the woman he swore high and low he loved. Was there news or a new lead?

Despite being the prime suspect in the case, there was absolutely nothing that proved he was the one who'd beaten Meri to death. Not even circumstantial evidence. No one could say for sure they'd seen him in the area, and no DNA had been found at the scene, not even fingerprints.

Before she could marshal her thoughts to reply, he went on to speak again.

"Is this where Chelsea and Kelly's party's at?"

This time suspicion won out. It wasn't beyond the deranged realms of Meri's ex to have arranged to have someone scope the house out to make a grab for the children. Willow periodically received threatening calls and messages from him, his family, and even some of his friends. Surely the policeman wasn't dirty? He'd seemed so decent, so trustworthy, so honest. She really hoped she was just being paranoid. Fear caused her to blurt out, rather rudely, "Why?"

Before he could reply, Willow heard a shriek behind her.

"Daddy!"

Willow turned in time to see one of the little guests, Gracie Dawson if she wasn't mistaken, hurtle past her and throw herself into the arms of the man standing on her doorstep. Laughing, he swung her up, giving her a big hug. The sound made her knees weak. Warm and rich, it could probably melt chocolate.

"Heya, pumpkin, whatcha been up to?"

"Daddy, you came."

"I promised you I would, didn't I?"

Not bothering to answer, she nodded, hugged him back and demanded to be put down so she could continue to run around with the other children. He put her down, seeing her attention had already shifted again, and watched as she ran off to join the other children inside.

Turning back, he grinned and said, "Sorry about that. I'm Gracie's dad, Adam."

"I – yes – um, Dawson – Adam Dawson. I

remember you." Willow took a moment to gather her scattered wits. "Yes, I gathered you might be her dad, after that rather enthusiastic welcome. I guess you pass the security test," Willow finally quipped in return. Inviting him in, she closed the door behind him. She guided him through the house to the patio where she'd been about to cut the cake.

"You're just in time to sing to the birthday girls."

Adam couldn't help but groan out loud. Turning to laugh at him, Willow took in his unrepentant shrug.

"Sorry, singing isn't my forte," he answered.

Clapping her hands, Willow called the children to gather round to sing to the twins while they blew out the candles on their cake. Hopefully, her shaking hands wouldn't give away just how deeply she was reacting to this man, not to mention the memories.

Making sure Gracie was securely strapped into

her car seat, Adam listened absently as she babbled on about the party. Since he mostly zoned out what she was saying, he didn't get all the details, but he certainly got that she'd had a fantastic time and that Aunty Willow was just the best. And could she "please, please, please" go play at Chelsea and Kelly's house again, "please?"

His thoughts were consumed by the woman he hadn't seen in three years. Willow Martin. It was strange how things worked out. The last time he'd seen her, he had been overwhelmingly attracted to her but unable to do anything about it. She'd been the complainant in an active investigation, and his captain would have had his balls if he'd so much as suspected the thoughts he'd been having about her.

Those very thoughts, of the woman who reminded him of a 1950s movie bombshell, now occupied his mind all the way home. Or rather, more accurately, all the things he'd love to be doing to her.

And with her. Maybe he could have a play date too. He wondered if she'd be game.

When they got home, he had an exhausted, ratty little girl on his hands. It was bath and dinner time, and if there was a God, bedtime. Gracie had never been an easy child when she was tired. One of the many reasons her mother had walked out on them, never looking back. Not that it was Gracie's fault. Her mother just wasn't worthy of being called one. Trisha was far more interested in herself and *her* needs than those of her husband or her baby.

Pulling himself up short, Adam focused on getting Gracie ready for her bath, so he didn't dwell on all the bitter thoughts of his self-absorbed, cheating ex-wife. She wasn't worth his time or effort. While keeping an eye on his daughter, he got dinner going. He had to admit, he was hungry and tired himself. He'd worked all day before picking up Gracie. Now he was ready for a bit of downtime. Maybe a beer and a sports game to watch.

Dinner over, dishes in the washer, Gracie tucked in tight for the night, Adam inhaled a deep sigh of satisfaction as he planted himself in his chair in front of the fifty-five-inch television he'd treated himself to on the day his divorce had been finalised. A celebratory gift to himself for getting rid of the miserable shrew. He still couldn't fathom how she'd so successfully fooled him into thinking she was the woman for him.

Surfing channels for a while, he couldn't find anything that grabbed his attention and found his thoughts drifting back to Willow. She unsettled him. He wasn't sure what it was about her, but while she gave off this "I am woman, hear me roar" vibe, there was something that lurked under the surface. Something vulnerable she didn't show the world. It called to him.

He'd been staring at the screen while thinking

about Willow, absently channel surfing some more. Action on the screen caught his attention, and he noticed he'd inadvertently stopped on the true crime channel. As he refocused on the television, his thoughts shifted to the case he'd been working that had brought her into his life.

Jumping up, he headed for his home office. A scratch through all his old notes and files would refresh his memory, but he remembered it had been an assault that had turned bad. So bad, in fact, the victim had succumbed to her injuries. The woman was Willow's friend, as he remembered it.

After a couple hours of rummaging around, he struck gold. The file he was looking for was buried pretty deep as it was now a cold case. The leads had dried up about three years ago, so it had been shelved in favour of more current cases. He grabbed himself another cold one before settling down to read through the notes he and Gavin had made on the case.

As he read, that night snapped into clear focus in his mind. He remembered the scene. Her friend, in an advanced stage of pregnancy, had left her physically abusive boyfriend. Pissed off about the situation, he'd paid her a visit at Willow's house to express his deep displeasure over her departure by beating her despite her being heavily pregnant with his children.

He'd left her for dead on the floor. Though Willow found her while she still barely clung to life, they'd been unable to save her. If the boyfriend had wanted her dead, he'd certainly gotten his wish. When the news had reached him that she'd died from her injuries, he'd gone on the run. There was also a note in the file about threatening phone calls Willow had been receiving, but they'd never been able to trace the calls back to the source as they'd always been made from stolen numbers.

Sitting back in his office chair, he got lost in thought as the events of that night and the following day unfolded in his mind's eye. Eventually, his thoughts circled back to the woman he'd seen today. Adam had seen the shadows that haunted those beautiful blue eyes of hers. The problem was, for the first time since his marriage had crashed and burned, he was interested in figuring out the story behind those shadows. He wanted to know what other harsh lessons life had handed her to cause such sadness. The thought freaked him out more than just a little.

Willow couldn't help but heave a huge sigh of relief. The craziness of the day was finally over, silence restored to the house once more. After all their guests left, she coaxed the girls into a quick shower and indulged their love of all things Disney by popping them down in front of the television to watch their current favourite princess movie. She even managed to get them to have a small, healthy snack before they finally succumbed to the excitement of the day, giving her an opportunity to clean up uninterrupted.

She carried the girls, one-by-one, to their room. Making sure the windows were tightly secured, she cast a last look at the girls as they slept peacefully before turning the light out, heading for the kitchen, and a well-deserved glass of wine. Not overly hungry, she put together a small cheese platter for herself. Taking her snack and wine, she made her way into the living room to take a load off.

The silence soothed her as she contemplated the day. She was thrilled the day had gone so well for the twins. In the first two short years of their lives, she'd been too scared to let them out of her sight, going so far as taking them to work with her every day. She'd found a nanny to look after the girls at her book store during the day, taking over their care in the evenings at home.

But not too long after their second birthday, she

realised she was doing more harm than good by giving in to her fears and insecurities. Pulling herself together, she found a day mother she felt comfortable with, who understood the need for security and who protected her girls almost as fiercely as she did.

Thoughts of those days inevitably brought about thoughts of Adam Dawson. His good looks and distinctive scar made his face one that was difficult to forget. Even though she'd been consumed by the grief and trauma of the situation, Willow hadn't been immune to the attractive detective. He was handsome and sexy, but more than that, he made her feel safe. Like she could trust him. And trust was not something that came easily to her. Her father had taught her early in life you couldn't trust people, sometimes not even loved ones, the day he'd walked out their front door and never so much as looked back, leaving her mother a broken and embittered woman.

Yawning, Willow stretched her tired muscles. Definitely time for bed. She made her way to the kitchen, putting her few dirty dishes in the dishwasher and headed for bed, too tired to bother with showering. Thankfully, she was almost as tired as her daughters and wouldn't struggle to find sleep.

Reaching over to her nightstand for her cell phone to set her alarm, she spotted the photo of Meri she kept there. God, she missed her friend. Her eyes ached with unshed tears as she thought back on the four years her best friend had missed out on with the babies that had meant everything to her. Meri had wanted nothing more from life than to be a mother. But her one chance at happiness had been brutally snatched from her.

Willow's thoughts circled back again to that time. Completely traumatised by how she'd lost one of the most important people in her life, she'd tried blocking the memories of that day in an attempt to just make it through each day. Grief had been an overwhelming, constant companion in the early days. At first, she tried to deal with it through counselling but eventually had given up.

The constant prodding and prying into pain too big to cope with had been more than she could stand at the time. So she abandoned therapy with intentions of going back at a later date. But eventually time had passed, and she'd gotten on with living a new life as best she could. She'd not had much choice since she'd taken custody of Chelsea and Kelly four months after their mother's death. They needed her whole and together. Or at least as whole and together as she could be.

The man who'd shown up on her doorstep today brought memories flooding back. Remembering him brought gut-wrenching pain, but she also remembered how gentle he'd been with her. When her world was coming apart, the compassionate police officer had offered her safe haven from a storm guaranteed to shred her. She'd never had the chance to thank him for showing her such kindness. For a while, she felt guilty about it, but she'd needed to forget, so she pushed all thoughts of that night deep down. And with it, all thoughts of Adam Dawson too.

Willow turned out the light and lay down. The tears she'd held back finally spilled over as the memories she'd fought for so long assailed her in the dark. Memories of the hunky detective, the only bright spot in the dark morass of recollection.

CHAPTER FIVE

Business was usually slow on Mondays. People detested having to go back to work after a fun-packed weekend. And since work was a necessary evil, they preferred to go straight home when their Blue Monday was done. Most likely to pour a big glass or two of their favourite wine while they tried to forget their craptastic day. Buying books most definitely wasn't high on their priority list for a Monday.

Her bookstore, The Reading Nook, had been her dream since she was a little girl. Reading was her passion. As a lonely child left to her own devices, reading offered an escape to exciting fantasy worlds far removed from her depressing one. In books, the father stayed with the mother, the mother loved her children, and the children were secure in the knowledge of that love. So, when it came to what she wanted to do with her life, it only made sense that it would involve books.

The quiet gave Willow plenty of time to think. Or maybe stress was a better way of looking at it. On her drive to work, she'd pondered the dilemma of tracking Adam Dawson down to invite him to dinner. She wanted to thank him, albeit three years late, for the kindness he'd shown her before. And if she was completely honest, she just really wanted to see him again. The dilemma came in that she had no idea whether he was single or not.

The man was indecently hot. No man had the right to be that sexy. The scar that ran down the one side of his face did nothing to detract from it either. In fact, in her opinion, it actually made him hotter. She couldn't help but wonder just how he'd gotten it.

Sitting in her office, her thoughts still firmly centred around the hot detective, her assistant wandered in to the back of the store, saving her from her thoughts.

Slender and tall, with midnight hair and sloe-eyes, Jade reminded her of an elegant ballet dancer as she entered the room.

"Everything all right there, Willow? You're looking somewhat put out," Jade laughed as she took in Willow's face.

"Just getting my panties in a bunch over nothing, Ms Nosy Parker," replied Willow, pulling a face, which had Jade giggling again.

"So, what's got you all bunched up then? Tell Aunty Jade. We'll fix you right up."

Willow studied Jade for a moment before answering her.

"I met someone at a very traumatic time in my life. At the time, he set my senses tingling, but as fate would have it, the timing was all wrong."

"Sounds intriguing. Do tell. What's changed?"

"The weirdest thing happened. He turned up at the house on Saturday. To fetch his daughter. How strange is that? That after all these years, he would just randomly reappear in my life like that?"

"Sounds like fate, all right! So, did he ask you out?"

Laughing at Jade's enthusiasm, Willow shook her head.

"No. I don't even know if he's single. I'm thinking about doing some digging to find out. Hence, my face looking like I drank vinegar. I'm driving myself crazy overthinking the situation."

"Don't overthink it then. Just go for it. What have you got to lose? If he's single, that is."

What indeed.

"I'll think about it."

"If you think about it for too long, you won't do

it. I say go for it."

As luck would have it, a mother and her young son wandered into the store at that moment, saving Willow from having to answer.

"This isn't over," Jade stage-whispered before going off to assist the customer. She threw a sassy grin over her shoulder as she walked away.

Willow couldn't help but laugh and shake her head. Jade was a good fit for her and the store. She was a bubbly, happy young woman with a zest for life that was a joy to behold. Being at the store, around Jade, never failed to lift Willow's spirits. In many ways, Jade reminded her of Meri. Maybe that's why she'd been so drawn to her when she'd applied for the assistant's position Willow had advertised.

Turning back to the matter at hand, Willow absently worried at her thumbnail. She'd already known he was a policeman. Now she knew he was the father of one of her children's friends too. She just didn't know anything else about him. Was he still married? Where was he stationed? Was he still at the same police station as three years ago, or had he moved to another? She could find out, but it meant asking around. That always got tongues wagging. With no other way to track him down, she would have to suck it up and ask.

Before she could chicken out, Willow dialled one of the mothers who'd befriended her when the girls had started day care the same day as her son. Hopefully, the search would begin and end with Candice. The call went to voicemail. Damn it. She hated talking to a machine.

"Hi Candy, it's Willow. I need your help with something. Please give me a call when you can? Thanks. Chat later."

She'd just have to wait a little longer it seemed. Her plan thwarted for the moment, she turned her attention back to the papers scattered all over her desk. Much as she wished for it, the paperwork wasn't going to do itself.

Adam's thoughts had been consumed by the Merida Davids cold case all day. It wasn't as if he didn't have current cases to keep him busy, but he couldn't get the case off his mind. He'd gone through all the notes he had at home and then looked up the file when he'd gotten to the office to see if there were more.

The details had all come back to him as he'd gone through his, Gavin's, and the uniformed officers' notes. Domestic abuse, dependence, and heartbreak had been the theme of the day. The case originally seemed like it would be aggravated assault or attempted murder as the victim was alive when she'd been found, but when she'd succumbed to her injuries, the public prosecutor escalated the charge to one of murder.

It was believed to have been the ex-boyfriend since there was a long history of violence, but nothing had ever been found that could tie him to the murder. At the time, a neighbour thought she'd seen him at the house that night, but in the end, she couldn't pick him out in a line up. She'd been unsure of her choice, finally picking the wrong person out. Eventually, Adam had to file it as a cold case when all leads ran dry. But he would never forget the scene. Merida was seven months pregnant when she'd endured her final beating.

She had fought hard to protect not only her own life but especially the lives of her unborn babies. Clearly, she had intended it to be her last beating but certainly not her final one. The chaos in the room had borne witness to that struggle for survival.

The case stayed on his mind for a long time after

it had gone to the archives. He wasn't sure why, since it had become routine early on in his career to deal with cases like that. Maybe it was because he'd been a new dad at the time and the victim was so highly pregnant. He suspected it had more to do with the victim's friend than the victim herself though. The delectable Ms Willow Martin.

The love she felt for her friend had been clear for anyone to see. The soft-spoken, soft-hearted Willow was devastated when her friend haemorrhaged to death on the operating table while delivering her babies.

A hearty slap on the back brought him out of his musings. Turning to see who it was, Gavin was taking a seat at his own desk. He and Gavin had been colleagues since the police academy training college but only partnered up when Gavin received his promotion to detective five years ago. As partners went, he couldn't ask for better. No matter what, he knew his friend had his back. Adam trusted the man with his life.

"Good morning. What you got there?" Gavin said.

"Morning. The Davids case file. Been giving it a go over."

"The Davids case?"

"Yes. Cold case from about four years ago. Assault with intent turned to homicide."

"Doesn't ring a bell. What's got you interested in it now?

"Gracie had a party this weekend. So I go to fetch her, and the mom opens the door. You could have knocked me over with a feather when I realised she was the complainant in the matter. The vic was her friend. The friend was staying with her after leaving her abusive boyfriend. Seems the ex didn't take kindly to his punching bag leaving, so he went around to the complainant's house to express his displeasure."

"Wait, wait. I think I remember it now. Vic was pregnant, wasn't she?"

"Yeah, that's the one."

"Yeah, those are always the ones that leave a nasty aftertaste. You got anything new?

"No. Was just going over the file to refresh my memory. Maybe we should see if we could fit time in to look into it again between the other cases?"

"Sure. Why not? Let me go through the case again. Maybe we can work a different angle. See what we can dig up."

Turning to current case files, they got down to catching up on paperwork.

The morning passed quickly. When Gavin stood up from his desk, Adam looked up enquiringly.

"Ready to grab a bite, bud?"

Adam nodded. "Give me a minute to log out."

Walking out of the office, Gavin asked, "So tell me about this lady that's got you digging. She pretty?"

Adam snorted.

"Trust you to think with your dick."

Shrugging unrepentantly, Gavin grinned. "Well, is she?"

"I'll tell you over lunch. Your turn to buy, lover boy."

James Jonson, or JJ as he was known to family and friends, stood outside the book store watching the woman standing at the counter. His hatred for her was ever present. He blamed her for all that was wrong in his life. She was the reason his beloved Meri was gone. Meri had always gushed on about Willow this and Willow that. When he'd met Meri, they had already been friends. Where one was, generally the other was too. Often, they'd made him feel left out.

A builder by trade, days were long and hard. It had infuriated him to no end coming home after a long day on a building site, only to find the two women laughing and lounging around but no supper prepared. If his mother had been there, he would have come home to a cooked meal and a bath ready for him to soak his tired muscles. There was so much his woman could have learned from his mother.

But instead, he had to put up with that bitch talking all kinds of crap into his sweet girl's head. She'd even been the one to convince Meri to leave him. When he'd needed to discipline Meri for her to see where she failed, she would run straight to her friend, crying abuse. And instead of sending her home, she finally convinced Meri to come to live with her instead. She should have just stayed out of their business. But she was going to get hers. He would make sure of it. His father had taught both he and his mother to stay out of a man's business, and they'd learned the lesson well.

He was coming for his babies. Taking back

what was his. His and Meri's. Something he should have done long ago. If he had, he wouldn't be in this miserable situation. All alone. Not to mention penniless. Once he had their children back, he'd have access to the money too. Although nobody knew that he knew, he'd found out about it. Now, he wanted his share. They owed him.

CHAPTER SIX

"Willow, hi."

"Hi. Thanks for returning my call."

Second-guessing herself, Willow wasn't sure she should go through with asking Candice for Adam's number. As much as she enjoyed interacting with the bubbly school mom, Willow was well aware it wouldn't take long for news of their phone call to become fodder for the gossip mill. Inherently a private person, that thought made her uncomfortable.

"It's all good, Wills. What's up?"

The moment of decision. She hesitated.

"Willow? You still there?"

"Sorry, Candy – still here. Got distracted for a

second." Taking a deep breath, she took the plunge. "Listen, I was wondering. Do you know Adam Dawson?"

"Sure, I know Adam. He's Gracie's dad. Hot and single, all the moms think he's just *all that*, you know? Why do you ask?" she answered with a laugh.

"He collected Gracie from the girls' party on Saturday, and I realised I know him from a few years back. I need to get in contact with him, and I was wondering if you have a phone number for me? Or know anyone who does maybe?"

"I don't have it, no, but I can get it for you. Give me a little time, and I'll get back to you later with the number."

Speculation was rife in Candice's tone, but at least she didn't come out directly and ask. Willow wasn't sure how she would answer. She was uncomfortable enough with the conversation as it was. But at least she now knew he was single. That she wasn't lusting after someone else's man.

"Thanks, doll. I appreciate it," was all she replied before changing the subject.

The women chatted for a while longer.

"All righty, doll, I've got to dash, but I'll get back to you later with that number. Have a fab one."

"You too, Candy. Thanks. Chat later."

Hanging up, she wasn't sure if it was trepidation or anticipation that had her heart beating a little faster.

Nerves still jumping, Willow picked up her phone and stared at it.

"It's not magically going to dial the number for you, you know," Jade teased.

Willow almost jumped out of her skin. She'd been alone in her office just seconds before. Giving Jade the evil eye, she turned back to her phone. If she'd hoped to get rid of her assistant with "the look", it had failed miserably. Jade laughed and pulled out the chair in front of her desk.

"Well, it's not. Want me to dial him for you?"

"What makes you think you know who I want to call? Or even if I'm going to call someone, Ms Smarty Pants?" Willow couldn't help the eyebrow that lifted, seemingly of its own accord. Her what-the-fuck eyebrow, as Jade called it.

Jade snickered, raising an eyebrow of her own.

"Doesn't take a genius to figure out why you're glaring at your phone."

Heaving a huge sigh of frustration, Willow tossed her phone back down onto her desk.

"Urgh . . . Why is this so hard? I mean, seriously? All I have to do is dial ten crummy numbers and have a conversation with the person on the other end. How hard is that?"

Willow pulled a face, and Jade cracked up.

"Oh my God, you're hopeless. I'll do it."

Before she could stop her, Jade had grabbed up the offending phone along with the piece of paper with the number and dialled before Willow could grab the phone back.

"It's ringing." Jade bounced in her seat.

She handed the phone back, and Willow gingerly put the phone to her ear. The other woman watched her closely. When her expression tightened, Jade was quick to ask, "What's the matter? Did he hang up on you?"

"No, it's gone to voicemail."

"Then leave a message."

Again, Willow pulled a face. She drew in a lungful of air, trying to quieten the butterflies in her stomach.

"Um . . . Hey, Adam. Hi. This is Willow – Willow Martin. I was wondering . . . Um, you know what? Never mind. I'll – I'll try again later."

Face flaming with embarrassment, she ended the

call, throwing the phone onto the desk in disgust. Jade, who had pointedly been ignoring her to this point, took one look at her face and cracked up all over again.

"I'm so glad you find this all so amusing," Willow said.

Holding a finger up, Jade tried to gather her composure. Just as she opened her mouth to reply to the rather grumpy comment, she made the mistake of looking over at Willow again. Her eyebrow was raised so high this time it seemed in danger of crawling all the way into her hairline. Jade couldn't hold back the laughter still bubbling beneath the surface.

Huffing in irritation over the whole thing, Willow jumped out of her chair.

"Wait, wait," Jade gasped. "I'm sorry. But your face is just so priceless. And that bloody eyebrow gets me every time."

As she opened her mouth to speak, Willow was

interrupted by the bell over the front door.

"Saved by the bell. Again." Jade grinned.

"I'll go see who it is," Willow answered, ignoring the comment, desperate to get away.

The sound of Jade's belly laugh followed her down the short passage into the shop.

Catching sight of the figure standing at the counter, Willow stumbled to a halt.

"Adam. Hi. What are you doing here?" she asked rather gracelessly.

She blushed, feeling stupid and awkward. As Adam went to speak, Willow held up a slender finger.

"If you laugh at me too, so help me, I swear I'll–I'll . . ." She broke off, throwing her hands up in the air in exasperation as she couldn't decide on what dire threat to make.

With a somewhat bemused look on his face, Adam replied, "No, ma'am. I wouldn't think of it."

Jade chose that moment to join them. She took

one look at Willow's face, looked over at the confused looking man standing by the counter and barely managed a choked "I'll be back" before fleeing the room as more laughter escaped from her.

"Seriously Jade?" Willow called after her but got no answer other than peals of laughter. Sighing again – it was all she seemed to be doing today – she turned back to Adam. Putting both hands up in mock surrender, he smiled.

"I seem to have a missed call from you. I was in the area, so I thought I'd just pop in and see what was up."

Oh, for the love of jelly beans. Shoot me now. I need to remember to murder Jade when I have no witnesses.

"Yes . . . um. Well, I thought, maybe . . ." She stumbled to an embarrassed stop. The dratted man clearly was enjoying this. He stood looking at her, waiting patiently. When she didn't continue, he took mercy on her.

"So, since I'm here, do you have time to grab a quick cup of coffee?"

Jade took that moment to re-enter the room.

"Go ahead, Willow. It's quiet today. I've got this."

Giving them a cheeky grin, she shooed them out the door, not giving Willow a chance to say no. An awkward silence settled between them as the door swung shut behind them and they found themselves standing outside.

"Well. Coffee it is then, I guess," Willow laughed after a moment.

Turning towards the coffee shop he'd seen as he entered the centre, he grinned back. He indicated for her to go ahead, and as they fell into step, he turned to look at her.

"I have a confession to make," Adam said.

"Yes?"

"Yup. Full disclosure. The reason I was in the

area is I was on my way to see you."

He watched a look of surprise shift across Willow's beautiful face before she could hide it.

"Oh. Really? Why?"

"Probably for the same reason you were looking for me? I wanted to see you again."

A subtle rose tinted her cheeks. He wasn't sure if she was embarrassed that he'd figured out why she'd called, or if she was reacting to the fact that he'd wanted to see her again. He really hoped it was the latter.

"I– ugh! Okay, fair's fair. Full disclosure." She took a moment, drawing in a deep breath. "I'm glad you did because I'm not sure I'd have had the courage to phone you back after being such a ditz in the voicemail."

"Well then, I'm glad I did, too."

They walked the rest of the short distance in an almost companionable silence, only a tiny hint of discomfort lingering. When they reached the coffee shop, he once again showed her to go ahead, and he followed her into the brightly lit open-plan space.

After having been shown to a table, the waiter took their order. As he left to place it, Willow looked around the space. They'd recently renovated, and this was the first time she'd been inside since. The bamboo and varying shades of green brightened the room and made the most of the natural light that flooded in through the wall of glass.

"I haven't been in since before they started the revamp here. They've done a really nice job with it," she said to break the silence that had settled over the table since the waiter walked away.

At her comment, Adam looked around the room too and nodded.

"Looks good."

They lapsed back into silence.

Seriously, Willow? The décor? That's what you're going to talk about?

Willow fidgeted with the salt and pepper shakers in front of her on the table, unsure what to say next. What had she expected him to say? As a policeman, she doubted décor interested him overmuch. Finally looking up from the shakers, she found Adam studying her. She shifted uncomfortably under the intensity of his scrutiny.

"Tell me something about yourself, Willow."

"Oh." She paused. She was just boring old Willow Martin. What could she possibly say that would make her sound anything other than that? In the end, she simply went with, "I can't say I have the most exciting story to tell, but okay, what would you like to know?"

"How about you start with why a book store, and we'll go from there?"

"The Reading Nook? That was always my dream,

to have my own book store. Books have brought such joy to my life, and I wanted to share that with others."

Anytime she spoke about books or her store, Willow lit up. She was passionate about anything to do with books. They'd been her escape during a lonely and mostly unpleasant childhood. They'd been her salvation. Adam's question broke the ice, and they chatted for ages, flitting from one topic to another – music, movies, family. Discovering, as they went, how much they had in common.

When a rare lull in conversation came up, Willow wracked her brain for something more to say. She wasn't quite ready to say goodbye. Then a thought popped into her head.

From the time she'd met him, Willow had been curious about Adam's scar. She briefly debated whether it was an appropriate time to ask or not, she eventually couldn't pass up the opportunity.

"It's a little personal, I guess, but I've been

wondering about how you got your scar." Her cheeks heated a little as she asked.

She watched as he stroked his fingers over the scar and swallowed. She wondered what they'd feel like stroking over her like that. Adam spoke, breaking into her reverie.

"When I was still a uniformed constable, my partner and I responded to a complaint of a disturbance. A homeless guy and his girlfriend were settling their domestic dispute with broken bottles. When I went to cuff the guy, his girlfriend came at me with her bottle neck. I wasn't quick enough to evade the blow, and my partner wasn't quick enough to stop her."

Willow simply stared. Her stomach pitched as she thought about how much it must have hurt, what a shock it must have been. And how differently it could have ended had his partner not intervened.

Inevitably, the conversation turned to

relationships, with Willow sharing that she'd never really been in a long-term relationship.

"Why not?"

She took a moment before answering. It wasn't something she'd shared with many people. In fact, Meri and the therapist she'd seen after Meri's death were the only two people who knew how deep her trust issues ran. Eventually, she spoke.

"It's not something I talk about, but my dad left us when I was about two months old. He never wanted children, but when my mother had my brother, it appeased his ego that he had a son to continue the family name." She took a sip of coffee, more as a means to bolster her courage than because she needed it. "But when I came along, he was not happy. At all. He stuck it out for two months before he decided the 'family life' was not for him, packed his bags, and left. She never heard from him again. Their divorce was dealt with through attorneys. She blamed me."

"Willow. I'm sorry. That must have hurt."

"You can't miss what you never had, right? But what did hurt was that my mother never let me forget that I was the reason he left. Bitter doesn't begin to scratch the surface of what my mother became."

"That sucks."

"Yeah, it does. But enough about me. What about you?"

It was Adam's turn to weigh his words.

"I met my ex-wife in my last year in police training. In the beginning, it was glamorous to have a police officer for a husband. Before Gracie came along, we spent a lot of time socialising, going places, being seen. Once she came along and Trisha realised that the easy freedom of movement was over, she became resentful – of Gracie, me, our life together. The shine wore off, I guess."

"So you got divorced?"

"Not before I caught her cheating on me with a colleague."

"No. Adam, that's horrible!"

"Clichéd, but true, I'm afraid." His smile was a touch depreciating. "I'm just grateful I got Gracie out of the deal. She didn't want her. Not even visiting rights."

"Who does that to their own child?" Willow burst out indignantly.

"People like her. Selfish, self-centred people."

The waiter chose that moment to come over to tell them they needed to start setting up for the dinner crowd.

"Oh, my goodness, Adam, look at the time. I need to get back."

"Yeah, I need to get going too. I'm surprised my phone's been so quiet. Come on then, I'll walk you back to your shop."

Adam took his wallet out of the back pocket of his jeans and counted out some bills, placing it in the bill folder the waiter had placed on the table with the check. He waited for Willow to gather up her handbag before walking her back to her shop.

Coming to a stop outside the book store, Adam turned to face her, giving her another one of his probing gazes before speaking.

"I had a great time this afternoon."

"I did too, Adam. Thank you."

"I'd really like to see you again."

"Yes, I'd like that too."

"I'll give you a call sometime then."

Not wanting to come on too strong, he leaned forward and placed a rather chaste kiss on her cheek before walking away.

CHAPTER SEVEN

Music played softly in the background. The bedtime routine of getting the girls down for the night done, Willow sank into the couch. Although it hadn't been a particularly busy day — Mondays were notoriously quiet — she was still tired. And the girls had been out of sorts this evening. She just hoped they weren't getting sick.

Taking a moment to savour a sip of wine, she reached for the stack of letters on the occasional table beside her. Flitting through mostly bills and junk mail, she came across a plain white envelope, only her name hand printed on the front. Curious as to what was inside, she rolled it over and slid a fingernail under the flap. She shook the contents out and then merely stared in shock.

Lying on her lap were three photos taken of her and Adam at the coffee shop earlier that day. A handwritten note lay underneath them. Reaching out a shaking hand, she lifted it and read.

I see you bitch. I didn't get my happy ending. You won't either.

Without conscious thought, Willow picked up her phone and dialled Adam's number as fear gripped her. He answered almost immediately.

"Hello?"

"Adam, hi. It's Willow. I'm sorry to bug you this late in the evening, but I don't know who else to call."

"Talk to me. What's going on? Are you okay? Are the girls okay?" His tone indicating he'd picked up on the distress in her voice.

"We're all fine. I was going through my mail and came across an envelope with my name written on the front. When I opened it, a note and three photos fell out. Of the two of us at the coffee shop earlier today."

"Try not to touch them too much. If you've got any, get them into a Ziploc bag or any plastic sandwich bag. I'm on my way."

Without another word, the phone went dead in her ear. She sat staring at it for a second, bemused at the abrupt end to the call. Tossing the phone onto the couch, she headed for the kitchen. She rummaged around in a drawer for a Ziploc bag big enough to put everything in. As an afterthought, she dug out a pair of latex gloves she kept on hand, for peeling beetroot she cooked for the girls so she wouldn't put anymore of her fingerprints all over the offending items lying on her couch.

Once she put the note and photos in the bag, she

sat back on the couch and threw back a healthy swig of her wine. She needed something stronger to calm her nerves, but since it was all she had, it would have to do. Besides, getting slammed wouldn't do her any good if the girls needed her during the night.

The sound of the doorbell cut through the silence, startling Willow. Dashing to the door, she quickly looked through the peephole to make sure it was Adam before opening it. Just seeing him standing on her doorstep helped settle her rattled nerves some. It was something she'd noticed about him before. Stepping back, she made space for him to enter.

"You okay?"

She simply nodded, not sure she could get words past the lump that had formed. He reached out and gently pulled her into a hug. She put her arms around his waist, sinking into the safety she felt there. They stood like that in the foyer for a long moment.

"Sure you're okay?"

"I'm better now," she finally managed.

For a moment longer, she luxuriated in the comfort of his embrace before stepping back a pace. Giving Adam a shaky smile, she headed for the living room.

"It's through here."

Adam followed her into the room. Standing near the door, she pointed to the plastic bag lying on her coffee table. Picking the bag up, Adam looked at the photo on top. He felt his gut tighten. Anger burned through him. It was when he turned the bag over, seeing the note inside, that it really took flame.

"Any idea who this could be from?"

He turned to look at Willow. Her eyes were huge with shock. Nerves showing as she stood worrying at a thumbnail. At first, it seemed as if she wasn't going to answer him, but then she spoke.

"It's only a guess, but I'd say JJ."

"To clarify, your friend's ex?"

"Yes."

"When I went through the file to refresh my memory the other day, I came across notations I'd made about threatening phone calls but nothing about written notes."

"Until now, it's only ever been verbal. This is the first time I've ever received a note."

Alarm bells rang in his head. These things had a habit of escalating. And it looked like he was now upping the ante.

As he stood looking at Willow, Adam realised he was going to have to take a step back from the case he'd just convinced Gavin to help him reopen. He'd wanted to help her find closure by solving this case, but as he stood looking at her, he realised that for the first time in a really long time he wanted to take a chance with a woman again. The very essence of her pulled at him, made him want her. That meant he'd have to choose. He couldn't be involved in an active investigation involving her and have a relationship with her. Making his decision, he spoke.

"I need to make a quick call. Give me a sec."

Dialling Gavin's number, he stepped to the window. Moving the curtain aside, he stared out into the lit garden, taking in the artful landscaping.

"Better be bleeding from an artery, bud. Otherwise, I might have to be the one to cause that bleeding."

Adam took a moment to absorb the sounds he could hear over the phone and realised he'd interrupted something. He couldn't help but chuckle.

"Sorry to interrupt the party, Casanova. The case we were talking about, the cold case? I'm going to need you to take over as IO. I'll tell you why another time. But that's not the reason I called. It seems we might have movement."

"Yeah? How so, bud?"

Gavin might like to play, but when it came to work, he was all in.

"The complainant in the case just received a threatening letter and some surveillance photos. She seems to think it might be from the suspect in the matter."

"Want me to come over?"

"Nah, I've got this. I'll book the evidence into the evidence locker on my way home. You get back to whatever it is I interrupted."

"All good. I'll see you in the morning."

"Yeah. See ya."

Putting his phone away, Adam turned to find Willow sitting on her couch staring at the photo that could be seen in the bag almost as if it were a snake ready to strike, she the unwilling victim. He walked over, and picking it up, he tucked it into the inner pocket of his jacket.

"I'm sorry! Where are my manners? I haven't

even offered you anything to drink." Willow jumped up. "What can I get you? A beer? I should have a beer in the fridge, I think. Or maybe some coffee? I can make some if you like."

"Coffee would be great, thanks. A beer would've gone down better, but I'm driving."

"Yes. Of course, yes. What was I thinking? Coffee it is. I'll be right back."

She dashed out of the room like the hounds of hell were on her trail.

Adam stared at the spot where Willow stood only a moment before. The shock now evident, adrenalin making her as jumpy as a Mexican jumping bean.

He followed her into the kitchen to find her frantically rummaging around in her freezer. He could hear her mumbling. Stepping closer, he heard her saying, "I know they're in here somewhere. Where the hell did I put them?" He was about to ask if he could help with anything when she spoke again.

"Yes! I knew they were in here."

Closing the door, she spotted him standing on the other side. She startled violently, clapping a shaking hand over her heart.

"Oh God! Adam, you scared me."

"Sorry. Didn't mean to. You sure you're okay?"

"Yes, of course. I'm fine. Let me grind these beans quickly, and I'll get that pot of coffee going."

He nodded. Thinking it best not to rile her up any further, he hopped up onto a barstool at the island counter, watching her. When the adrenalin subsided, she was going to crash, and he doubted it would be pretty. The whirring of the grinder started up, preventing any further conversation for the moment. The beans done, Willow set the coffee maker to percolate, avoiding looking at him.

"Willow?"

Still not looking his way, she murmured a "Hmm?" so softly he nearly didn't catch it.

"Willow, look at me."

She dropped her head but still didn't turn around. Slipping off the stool, Adam went over to where she stood. Laying a hand on her shoulder, he gently nudged her around to face him, almost like he was coaxing a child. When she was turned, he tucked a finger under her chin. She finally lifted her gaze to meet his.

"It'll be okay. Gavin and I will make it so. I won't let anything happen to you or the girls."

Her full bottom lip quivered. Biting down on it, she stilled the movement. Although she finally stood still, her body still vibrated with nerves, her fingers flexing, as if she needed to be fiddling with something to occupy them. She nodded but never said a word.

Adam watched as emotions flitted over her face. An expressive face. He reckoned she'd be crap at poker since her countenance pretty much gave voice to her emotions, even when she never spoke a word.

He found that refreshing and, quite frankly, arousing. Then again, it wasn't just her lack of artifice he found enticing. If he was brutally honest, most everything he'd seen of her so far stoked him. Now wasn't the time to do anything about it, but he also felt a strong need to comfort her. The coffee maker gurgled, indicating it was done. She stepped back to attend to the machine, and the moment was lost.

The note had completely freaked Willow out. She hadn't known who else to turn to other than Adam. Now that he was here, besides her jumping nerves, her senses were starting to hum too.

She'd come to the kitchen to make coffee to settle her nerves, and he'd followed her into the room, watching her without saying a word. Seeing too much.

Now, standing in front of Adam, she desperately wanted him to take her in his arms. She wanted to feel anything but the fear that had become so much a part of her life in these past four years with JJ terrorising her. But this was bigger than that. More than anything, she just wanted him. He made her feel things no man ever had.

Men were not trustworthy. This was Monica Martin's embittered viewpoint after Willow's father had abandoned them, and she had taken every opportunity to drill this lesson into her young and impressionable daughter. Willow learned her lessons well. The only man she had ever trusted was her brother, Brett. Until she'd met Adam.

She wasn't sure what it was about him that made her feel she could count on him, but she did. It melted her heart seeing how he'd been with his daughter, Gracie, when he'd collected her from the twins' party.

But it was more than that. He had a way of looking at her that made her burn, made her long for him to touch her, to taste her. He called to all that was feminine in her. She wanted so much for him to take her into his arms. When the coffee machine ruined the moment, she could have howled out her disappointment.

Adam watched as Gavin dropped down into his desk chair, noting the evidence bag in his hand.

"I see you got the letter."

"Yep. Wanna clue me in? That was a badly timed cryptic call last night, by the way."

Adam laughed, shaking his head at his friend. Gavin was a notorious ladies' man, proclaiming he wasn't ready to settle down yet.

"Simple, my man. Willow Martin received that letter in her mailbox last night."

Adam nodded his head at the letter in the other man's hand. Gavin studied Adam for a moment before he answered.

"Yeah, I got that bit. How about you tell me the bit about me taking over as IO. When I had to go for my shoulder op at the time of the incident, it was given to you. Now you want to give it back? Any particular reason?"

The speculative look on Gavin's face gave Adam pause. Was he that obvious? Or was it just that his partner knew him that well?

"Conflict of interest, my friend. Gracie and her kids are friends. I'm personally involved now. Ergo conflict of interest."

Shaking his head, Gavin grinned.

"Ergo, my ass. There's more to this story than meets the eye, bud. I smell a rat. But since I'm such a nice guy, I'll let it go for now. However! As punishment for holding out on me, my conditions are straightforward. One of my cases for that one."

"Fair enough. What you got for me?"

Rooting around on his desk, Gavin found the file

he was looking for. He tossed it over to Adam with an evil grin.

"Have at it. This one's all yours now."

Looking down at the file he'd caught mid-air, Adam groaned as he saw it was the file for a spate of armed robberies targeting lingerie stores across the peninsula. His partner just laughed. The owner of the chain being targeted was difficult and mean-tempered, and no one wanted to deal with her. Gavin had been stuck with the case since he couldn't get anyone to swap out with him.

"Bastard," Adam muttered.

"Don't kid the kidder, dude," came the laughing retort.

"Yeah, yeah. Whatever."

It was going to be a long day.

CHAPTER EIGHT

Willow waited patiently as the two chattering little girls clambered into the car. She always made sure they buckled themselves into their car seats properly. Sometimes she worried she was overly protective of the girls, but they were all she had now. Her brother, Brett, lived in New Zealand – too far away for much more than the occasional call or message.

"Mommy, are you even listening to us?" Chelsea asked, somewhat put out by Willow's nonresponse.

"Sorry, angel pie. Mommy missed that. What did you say?"

Her long-suffering sigh had Willow biting back a smile.

"Chelsea asked if we could invite Gracie Dawson over to come to play this weekend. Please, Mommy?" Kelly replied instead.

"I didn't know you girls were such big friends. You've never talked much about her before."

"She was at our party. Don't you remember?" Chelsea said.

"Yes, I remember. But I don't remember you talking about her much."

"She's kinda new at school. We like her 'cos she's always nice to us," Kelly chimed in.

"Sure. Why not? I'll phone her dad to ask."

"Did you know she doesn't have a mommy anymore? Her mommy ran away from her and her daddy when Gracie was a baby. You wouldn't ever do that, hey Mommy?" Chelsea looked earnestly at her mother as she asked.

Before she could reply, Willow had to swallow past the lump that had formed in her throat. She shook her head as she looked into their sweet little faces.

"No, my babies, I would never run away from you. Mommy loves you too much to ever run away from you."

Satisfied with the answer, the two girls went back to their own conversation again. For Willow, it was a tad bit harder to move on from. She felt for Gracie. For Adam. To have Trisha up and leave them like that must have been hard. She couldn't begin to imagine what Adam had gone through trying to raise his daughter on his own, especially with his job. It didn't take long, however, for one of the twins to circle back around to the topic of Gracie coming over to play.

"Mommy, will you phone Gracie's dad when we get home to ask if she can come play on Saturday, please?"

"Yes Chels, I'll phone him."

"Promise?"

"Yes, Chelsea. I'll phone once you've had your wash and supper, okay?"

"Okay," the girls chimed together.

Their happy chatter filled the car for the rest of the short trip home, never stopping. Not even when she pulled into the garage and they headed into the house.

Hugs and kisses and bedtime stories over, Chelsea and Kelly snuggled down to sleep. Smoothing a hand over their heads, Willow placed one last kiss on each forehead, savouring the moment. Appreciating it more than usual.

"Night rascals. I love you."

"Night, Mommy. Love you too," Chelsea replied.

"Night, Mommy. Love you," Kelly echoed.

Turning out the light, Willow headed for the living room and a glass of wine to unwind. Before she reached the end of the passage, a little voice rang out.

"Please don't forget to phone Gracie's dad. Please, Mommy."

Smiling to herself, she answered, "Yes, Kelly. Now go to sleep, please. Love you."

"Love you more," she heard Kelly reply.

"Nope, *I* love *you* more."

She heard a giggle and then, "Nope, me."

"Now don't start that again."

More giggling and then, "Love you the mostest," chorused out.

Willow grabbed her cell phone on her way to the living room. She'd best get on with phoning Adam. She'd promised the girls, and there would be no rest for her soul if she didn't. Her daughters would simply nag until it was done. Besides, it gave her an excellent excuse to phone the man. There was no denying that slight rasp in his deep voice did things to her – made her sadly neglected libido sit up and pay attention.

Checking the time to make sure it wasn't too late to call, Willow dialled Adam's number. She listened to it ring as she mentally rehearsed what she would say to him when he answered.

"Willow, is everything okay?"

"Hi, Adam. Yes, we're fine thanks. I'm actually phoning about Gracie."

"Gracie?"

"The girls were wondering if she could come over for a play date on Saturday."

"Sure. No problem. Do you want me to drop her off or will you be fetching her?"

"Well, I thought I could pick her up, and you could collect her, maybe stay for dinner?" There was a beat of silence from Adam, making Willow's heart sink. "Of course, if you've already got plans, I completely understand."

She slapped a hand against her forehead. What had she been thinking? She'd probably completely misread any interest she thought he might have shown. As smoking hot as he was, she was sure he didn't lack for female attention.

"Actually, I was thinking I'd really like that. It's a rare thing to have a beautiful woman offer to make me dinner."

Was it her imagination, or did his voice sound huskier than usual?

"Really?" she blurted, not at all expecting his reply. "Sorry, that sounded so rude. I only meant I can't see how someone as smoking hot as you wouldn't have offers a-million."

Willow clapped a hand over her mouth, flushing bright red. Clearly, the filter between her brain and her mouth was malfunctioning tonight. *God, what an idiot! Could I possibly be any more gauche?* As he laughed at her words, the sound of his amusement washed over her. Whether he was talking or laughing, his voice was lethal. It hit her straight in the heart of her femininity, making her core tighten.

"So, you think I'm smoking hot, do you?"

Embarrassment riding her hard, Willow didn't know how to respond.

"Cat got your tongue, honey?" His voice still held a broad trace of humour. "Would it help if I told you I think you're smoking hot too?"

"Oh Adam, you don't have to say that. You don't have to make me feel better about humiliating myself."

"Why would you think I don't find you hot?"

"Because I have a mirror?"

"Then I'm thinking you have a faulty mirror. Or eyesight. But let me tell you, there's nothing wrong with *my* eyesight. I see you, and I like what I see."

"Wow. I just– wow. I don't know what to say to that."

"Just say, 'Thank you, Adam'."

It was Willow's turn to laugh.

"Just say thank you, Adam."

"Touché, funny lady."

It felt good to be joking and enjoying the attention of a man. It had been a long time since she'd felt *any* kind of spark. Sure, they flirted and chatted her up at the book shop or on the rare occasion she went out with her girlfriends. But it had been too long since she'd been inclined to explore the possibilities. She couldn't help laughing at and with Adam. His sense of humour appealed to her. But then again, there was a lot about him that appealed to her. On the other hand, she didn't see herself quite the way he saw her. She'd never considered herself particularly attractive, and especially not sexy. As it made her uncomfortable, she needed to steer the conversation in a different direction. She started chatting to him about the plan for Saturday, his and Gracie's food tastes, and what time she'd pick Gracie up.

"Does six thirty suit you for dinner?" she

continued.

"Yeah, six thirty's good. I'm on standby on Saturday, so there's a chance I could get called away, but I'm really looking forward to it."

"I am too." She got butterflies just thinking about it. "It's getting late though, so I'm going to say good night and head for bed. Night, Adam."

"Yeah, I'm pretty worn out myself. I reckon I'll head for bed too. I'll see you Saturday. Night, honey."

Hanging up the phone, Adam groaned out loud. He now had the image of a naked Willow stuck in his head. A very hot naked Willow. God, just the thought of it had him hard. In his mind's eye, he imagined being the lucky guy who got to watch her undressing for bed. He liked how she dressed – she tended to choose clothing that enhanced her curves in all the right places, showed a little bit of skin while leaving most of it to the imagination. Though he had a pretty good imagination, he'd far rather he got to see what was under her clothes.

He wondered what she wore beneath the understated yet sexy outfits she wore. Was Willow into practical, plain cotton, or was she a lingerie kind of girl? Just the mental picture of her in silk and lace almost had him groaning again. He'd never been one for flights of fancy or daydreaming, but he could sit and daydream about getting the delectable Ms Martin naked and sweaty all day long.

It had been a long day. Right then, he was damn tired, but how the hell was he supposed to get any sleep with a hard-on that could shatter cement? That's what fantasising about Willow in nothing more than skimpy underwear and fuck-me heels did to him. If he had a hope of getting any sleep, he was going to have to take himself in hand and relieve the tension. He'd far rather be doing something about it with Willow, but he'd have to settle for the fantasies in the meantime.

After making sure the house was locked up tight and the alarm set for the night, Willow headed for her bedroom. The conversation with Adam played like a song on repeat in her mind. It gave her self-esteem a boost to think Adam found her desirable. Growing up, her mother had always been hyper-critical of her. She had always made Willow feel small and insignificant, dull and unwanted. The older woman had ingrained it in Willow from early on that no man would ever want her.

When Willow's father walked out, it had turned her mother bitter, and she'd used that deep well of poison very effectively, eroding trust of the male species in her young daughter. Willow had been a sponge, absorbing the embittered woman's indoctrination. But Adam inspired a sense of trust she'd never experienced in her life before. She wanted to be with him, and she was willing to put herself out there, to take the risk. Saturday would be the perfect opportunity. She just hoped she wasn't setting herself up for rejection because she'd read the signs wrong.

Although she'd dated on and off over the years, she'd never had a long-term, serious relationship. Not to mention, sex was now a distant memory for her. She couldn't remember when the last time was she'd enjoyed a warm body rather than the disinterested attention of a battery-operated device. While a vibrator scratched the surface itch, it didn't cuddle after or tell her that she'd rocked its world. She craved a human touch – specifically, she craved Adam's touch. But for tonight, it would just be her trusty old B.O.B. and her X-rated fantasies of Adam.

CHAPTER NINE

Had three days ever dragged by *so slowly* in the history of time? Willow didn't think so. She wasn't sure who was more excited for Saturday to arrive – her or the twins. Each evening, they'd regale her with the plans they'd been making with Gracie that day. The only thing that made the wait bearable was that Adam had taken to phoning her in the evenings. They'd spent hours talking in the last few days. And the more she got to know Adam, the more she wanted to know.

Finally, Saturday dawned bright and temperate, as only a gorgeous autumn's day in Cape Town could. The twins had been up even earlier than their already almost-inhumanely early time. They were now on their way to pick up Gracie for their picnic and playtime at the ever-popular Bugz Bar near the charming little town of Stellenbosch. The girls had been nagging to go for weeks, so Willow figured it was as good a place to spend the day as any.

There was plenty to keep the three children entertained while she could catch up on her reading. The park had staff constantly keeping an eye on the children as they played, and security was tight enough that the girls could play without her having to watch them like a hawk all day. A feature that was a huge draw card for the paranoid mother in Willow, especially when it came to her girls.

They set up under a shaded spot to shield them from the harsh African sun. While all three girls went off to get their faces painted, Willow stretched out on the blanket with her book, keeping an eye on them from where she lay. With a wide selection of activities to choose from, they found plenty to keep them occupied, only coming back to her for a new application of sunscreen or something to drink.

Lunchtime rolled around, and the picnic lunch Willow had packed was devoured by three very hungry pre-schoolers. Taking an opportunity to get a word in as they lay on the blanket in the shade, Willow reminded them that they had an hour left before it was time to head for home to start preparing dinner. A collective moan went up until Willow reminded them Adam would be joining them and expected to be fed.

The thought of "mommy's new friend" coming over was enough to pacify them for the moment. They dashed off to get some last-minute playtime in, and Willow went back to her book – a much-anticipated finale in one of her favourite erotic romance series. But eventually, it was time to head for home. She gathered up their gear and collected the little ones.

Excitement was starting to build. In just a couple of hours, she'd get to see Adam. She couldn't wait.

Completely tuckered out from running around all morning, the girls asked if they could watch a movie. Since there was only one they ever seemed to want to watch lately, she popped it in and got them settled before heading to the kitchen to make dinner. She'd decided on a simple lasagne and salad since it required little attention once it was all put together.

The doorbell rang at the same time she bent to put the lasagne in the oven. Three little voices yelled out to let her know there was someone at the door. Smiling in amusement, Willow closed the oven before going to answer the front door. Nervousness and excitement churned uncomfortably in her stomach, vying for first place.

As she walked past the living room, she heard singing about "letting it go" coming from the movie the girls were watching for the second time since they'd gotten home. It was beyond her how they weren't sick of this particular movie, especially since her two watched it so often she could probably do voiceovers for it herself.

Willow checked her reflection in the mirror beside the front door, just to make sure her hair wasn't a ringer for Medusa and she didn't have some kind of ingredient smeared on her face. Seeing she wasn't likely to scare small children or animals, she opened the door. A freshly showered, divine smelling Adam stood on her doorstep with a beautiful bunch of brightly coloured tulips and a panty-melting smile firmly in place.

"Hi. Come on in." Willow stepped out of the way with an inviting smile.

"Hi, yourself," Adam greeted, handing the flowers to her as he stepped across the threshold. "These are for you."

"Brownie points for the flowers, Mr Dawson.

Flowers are always a winner in my book. And bonus points for them being my favourite too."

Executing a shallow bow, Adam grinned again.

At the smile, Willow narrowed her eyes and asked, "How *did* you know they were my favourite anyway?"

Laughing outright this time, Adam shrugged.

"Simple. I phoned Jade. I figured the chances of her knowing were good."

Giving him a sassy grin she said, "I'll award you extra bonus points for the great detective work, Detective."

His good humour was infectious. Leading him down the passage, she stopped at the living room, indicating with a finger the little bodies sprawled over the living room floor.

"Hey pumpkin, whatcha up to?" Adam asked Gracie.

"Hi, Daddy. We're watching a movie. Wanna

come watch with us?"

Pulling a horrified face while giving a mock shudder, Adam declined.

"You're funny, Daddy," was all he got for his effort before Gracie went back to watching the movie.

"Girls, aren't you going to say hello?"

As one, Chelsea and Kelly chorused a greeting before turning their attention back to the movie too.

"Can I get you something to drink since that seems to conclude tonight's greetings?"

"Sure. I could slay a cold one, but unfortunately, I'm on standby. I'll have something cold though if you have it."

Willow led Adam out onto the patio before going to the kitchen for their drinks. When she returned, she found him standing at the railing taking in the spectacular view before them. The patio faced the majestic Table Mountain and afforded a panoramic view of Table Bay. Even the Green Point Stadium, where the 2010 soccer World Cup had been hosted, graced their view.

She handed Adam a soda and settled down on one of the sofas with her glass of wine. Thanking her, Adam came to sit beside her. Easy conversation flowed until Willow looked at her watch and realised it was bath time. She had about thirty minutes to get them in and out of the tub before dinner time.

"I'm going to get the girls into the bath before dinner. Can I get you another soda before I go?"

"I'm good thanks. You go ahead."

Dinner over and the kitchen put to rights, they'd played Snap at the kitchen table for a short while before the busy day finally caught up with the little ones. Now with the girls sleeping, the quiet of the autumn evening settled around Willow and Adam as they sat, side-by-side, on the patio sofa. The tension hummed between them. It had been building all evening, and Willow was about to come out of her skin. Lost in her thoughts, she started as she felt a gentle hand slide under the long hair she'd worn down for the evening, and settle on the back of her neck.

She turned to look at Adam to find his eyes already on her. The look in them had her feeling edgy. His intense gaze roamed over her face, taking her in, missing nothing. Willow licked lips gone dry, and that gaze dropped to watch the movement.

"Do I make you nervous, Willow?"

Hesitantly, she nodded.

"Why?"

"I'm so out of my depth with you, Adam."

"Ah, honesty. I like it. By now, you've figured out I'm a straight shooter. I say what's on my mind; no beating around the bush. What you see is what you get."

Again, Willow nodded.

"If there's something you want to know, ask me. If there's something on your mind, talk to me. Why are you out of your depth with me?"

She looked away, taking in the beautiful vista of lights coming on in the Mother City spread out before her, and took a moment to gather her thoughts. They raced through her mind as she tried to decide how much she felt comfortable revealing. Taking a deep, fortifying breath, Willow spoke.

"I don't know what the rules of engagement are in this situation. I don't have a lot of experience with men in general. I don't know what you want from me in particular. And that makes me feel out of my depth." Turning back to him, she looked directly into his eyes. Curiosity getting the better of her, she asked boldly, "What do you see when you look at me, Adam?"

Adam shifted, so he was angled towards Willow, mirroring the way she sat facing him. Showing no signs of shying away from the look or the question, he slid his hand up to cradle the back of her head, never breaking eye contact.

"I see a woman with a beautiful heart and a face to match. I see a woman with a body built to please a man. And full disclosure, honey, I want to be that man."

He certainly didn't beat around the bush. Willow's heart stuttered in her chest. The look in Adam's eyes had turned heated. He sat forward, leaning into her space. His eyes holding hers, he lowered his head until his lips barely touched hers.

"Adam, I—" Lost for words, Willow stumbled to a halt, worrying at her bottom lip with her teeth.

Closing the tiny gap, Adam used his teeth to pull the abused lip between his own and sucked on it softly. Sensation arrowed straight through Willow, her whole body tightening in response. Unconsciously, she leaned into the motion. Adam groaned low in his throat before pulling her in for a kiss. Sliding his other hand into her hair, he cradled the sides of her head between his large palms. Her lips parted for him, and his tongue swept in, stroking hers.

Willow's senses swam. She felt surrounded by Adam. She inhaled him – the smell of his cologne, his shampoo, the scent she recognised as uniquely Adam. She felt him – the strong, steady thump of his heartbeat under her hand as it lay on his chest. And God, she tasted him – he tasted of coffee and desire.

Tilting his head a little more, Adam deepened the kiss. Willow responded by sucking gently on his tongue, making him groan again. Was it possible to combust from the heat of a kiss? Because if it was, she was sure it might just happen in that moment. Her core tightened. She couldn't remember ever wanting a man like this.

Adam's hand moved over her slowly, appearing to savour the silken texture of her smooth skin beneath his fingertips. Reaching her breast, he moulded his hand around it, scraping a thumbnail over the tightly beaded nipple. At her low moan, he repeated the gesture.

Gathering her closer, Adam kneaded her breast, raining kisses on her face and her neck. Like her, his breathing was ragged; it seemed she wasn't the only one affected by this sensual onslaught. Willow felt a rush of moisture between her thighs as Adam latched his teeth onto a highly sensitised nipple over her top. She couldn't hold back the whimper of pleasure escaping her lips. Resting his forehead against hers, Adam seemed to need a moment to reign in his uneven breathing.

"I ache for you so badly right now. Am I moving too fast here? I don't want to scare you."

"God, Adam, I feel like I'm ready to combust. Even if we *are* moving too quickly, I'm not sure I could wait any longer."

Lifting his head, his gaze seemed to see all the way into her soul.

"I want to be with you tonight, honey. Here, now."

Holding his gaze, Willow nodded. Reaching for the hem of her strappy top, she pulled it up over her head, revealing the sheer, purple lace bra she wore. Adam ran his fingertips across the pale flesh above the top of its cup. As he leaned in for another kiss, his phone vibrated in the back pocket of his jeans, intruding harshly on the moment.

Despite feeling equally put out, Willow couldn't help but smile at Adam's bad-tempered cursing as he pulled the offending instrument out of his pocket. She watched as he took in the number on the screen of his phone before he cursed again.

"I'm really sorry, Willow. I have to take this, honey. It's work."

"Go ahead and get it. I'll go check on the girls

while you take your call."

Suiting action to word, Willow rose from the sofa as she heard Adam growl into his phone, "Yeah, Dawson."

Finding all well with the sleeping children, she returned to the patio to find Adam pacing like a caged panther. Willow took a moment to savour the grace with which he moved. He turned to pace back and caught sight of her standing in the doorway. By the look on his face, she knew before he even said a word that their wonderful evening was over.

"I'm so sorry to have to cut and run, but I'm needed at work." Rubbing a hand over the back of his neck, he hung his head as if there was something more he wanted to say. Eventually, he looked up again and simply said, "I'll go get Gracie and be on my way."

Disappointment washed through her, but to be fair, she'd known that this was a possibility.

"You don't have to do that, Adam. Really. There's no need for you to wake her and your parents. It's fine for her to stay here."

He walked over to where she still stood in the doorway and pulled her fully out onto the patio and into his arms.

"I really am sorry, honey. You have no idea how badly I want to stay here with you, but this is my job."

"I understand. Honestly. Yes, I'm disappointed, but this is what you do, and I knew that. It's all good. Don't worry about it. Just go do what you need to do."

Dropping a kiss on her forehead, Adam drew her in for a quick hug.

"I'll just go say goodbye to Gracie then if you're sure it's no hassle."

"Absolutely. She's welcome here."

Having said goodbye to his daughter, Adam followed Willow to the front door. Standing with a hand on the door handle he leaned in for one last kiss.

"This isn't over. You and me, we're going to happen, Willow. Sooner rather than later. You with me on this?"

"I'm with you, Adam. It'll happen."

Pulling the door open, he stepped onto the front porch.

"I'll give you a call in the morning to make arrangements to come get Gracie. Sleep well." Adam ran a fingertip across Willow's plump bottom lip. "Sweet dreams."

"Be safe, Adam."

Willow watched Adam walk to his car.

When he reached it, he turned to get in. He must have noticed her standing there because he said, "Go on in and lock up, honey. I'll wait."

"Okay. Night, Adam."

Once she'd done as instructed, she went to

the living room window overlooking the drive and waved to Adam who stood watching the front of the house. She returned the brief wave he gave before he got into his car and left. She knew his crime scene awaited.

JJ looked around the room. It held everything he imagined four-year-old girls would want. He'd been watching and waiting, biding his time, but he couldn't afford to wait anymore. Not now that the policeman was on the scene. He couldn't have foreseen that development. But he wasn't letting it put him off.

He was sick of watching that stuck-up bitch raise his and Meri's daughters. If she thought she was going to get her hands on Meri's money through their kids, she was sadly mistaken. They were his, as was the money. And he was determined to take it all back.

It still burned him that Meri had never once said a word about the grandmother with the inheritance. He had broken his back to give her a nice home and buy her pretty things when all along she had money that would have made life a hell of a lot easier on them all. It was pure coincidence that he'd found out. A letter from her attorney had arrived for her after she'd already moved out.

He'd been so mad at her the day he'd gone to see her at Willow's house. First, she'd lied to him, by omission sure, but a lie, nonetheless. And then she'd left him, taking his babies with her. But the worst insult was when she'd refused to see him. After everything he'd done for her, she thought she could just cut him out of her life and never give him another thought? Not bloody likely.

JJ had just wanted to teach her a lesson – she was always repentant after he'd given her a "lesson." But that day, she had remained steadfast in her refusal to come home. By the time he'd realised he'd gone too far, it was too late. Meri just lay there, unmoving. He'd panicked and run, leaving her bleeding on the floor.

In his mind, he believed Meri was responsible for her own death. Her and her meddling friend. If she had just heeded him and not listened to Willow, Meri would still be alive and well, living a life of luxury with him and raising their beautiful girls. Instead, he was all alone and broke. It was no way for a man to live. But not for much longer.

He was going to get back what was his and disappear. Head for somewhere with no extradition treaty and live out the rest of his days never having to watch his back again. It meant he would have to make his move now though before the policeman became more of a fixture in their lives and complicated everything even more.

Giving the room one last quick look, JJ headed

for the door. His new future beckoned.

CHAPTER TEN

Energy restored after a good night's sleep, pandemonium reigned. The girls were so excited to have woken up to find Gracie still there, they were now tearing around the house laughing and shouting and playing tag. It still astounded Willow how such little bodies could produce so much noise. She suspected the fact that they'd be spending another day together had a lot to do with it too.

Adam phoned to invite them on a drive around the peninsula with a stop for lunch somewhere along the route. And the girls weren't the only ones excited. The thought of spending the day with Adam appealed to her immensely. To be honest, *he* appealed to her immensely.

Willow had always been happy with her own company. It was the one thing she and Meri had never agreed on. She'd never understood her childhood friend's need for a man in her life. If Meri wasn't in a relationship, she complained she felt incomplete. Having been taught early that she couldn't trust men, Willow had been happy to live her life without one.

She'd never actively sought out a man, nor had any of her short-lived romances convinced her that her mother was wrong. But everything about Adam screamed reliability and trustworthiness. Not to mention how dedicated he was to his daughter. The daughter he had brought up on his own from little more than a new-born when his wife had turned her back on them both to pursue a life without them.

Adam had stepped up, doing an amazing job of making his daughter feel loved and secure. The very opposite of Willow's own mother. Willow admired him for it. It made her believe that maybe not all men were like her father.

Shouts of excitement broke into Willow's thoughts. A litany of "He's here, he's here" rang out as she made her way to the front door to let Adam in. Little bodies milled around her, jumping up and down in anticipation. As she opened the door, Gracie launched herself at her father. He caught her up in a hug as she shouted happily, "Yay Daddy, you're here! We've been waiting for you forever."

Blowing a raspberry in the child's neck, he laughingly replied, "I can see you've grown old waiting for me. Just look at all that grey hair."

Little girl giggles greeted his proclamation. Gracie wriggled to be let down and raced off with the twins when he obliged. He straightened up and gave Willow his panty-dropping smile.

"Good morning, gorgeous."

"Good morning yourself, handsome."

Closing the door behind him, he leaned in to give her a quick kiss, but the moment his lips touched hers, and she sighed, he couldn't resist pulling her in for a more thorough kiss. As he deepened it, they heard gagging sounds.

"Eww, they're kissing."

"Gross."

"Eww, kissing. Yuck"

"I guess that's our cue to get going then." Adam snorted with laughter.

Adam got the twins' car seats from Willow's car and got all three little girls strapped in while Willow closed the house, making sure everything was turned off, and the windows and doors were secured. When she stepped out onto the front porch, Adam stood waiting for her at the passenger door of his SUV.

Movement off to the side caught Willow's eye, and she turned her head to look, her hand freezing in mid-motion of locking the front door, shock slapping hard at her. On the other side of the road stood a man she could swear was JJ. Adam noticing her jolt called out, asking if she was okay.

She turned to look at him briefly before looking back to where JJ stood. But looking back, the man was gone. Surely, it couldn't have been a figment of her imagination, could it have? She was sure she had seen him. Adam jogged over to where she stood immobile.

"Are you okay? You look like you've seen a ghost."

"Did you see the man standing on the other side of the road?" Willow asked urgently

Adam looked in the direction Willow pointed.

"Man? No. I didn't see anybody. Who did you see?"

Willow looked to the opposite side of the road again. She was so sure she'd seen JJ standing there. But clearly, she was wrong.

"I must have been seeing things," she replied.

"We should probably get going."

Adam gave Willow what she called his "detecting" look but decided to leave things be. He cast one last look in the direction she'd pointed before directing her to precede him to the car where the children were starting to get impatient.

Climbing behind the wheel, Adam started the car and backed down the drive. Willow felt well and truly shaken but didn't want to spoil the day, so she pasted a smile on her face. Thankfully, the children were oblivious to the drama.

It was a thirty-minute drive from the northern suburb of Plattekloof to the small fishing village of Hout Bay. Willow soaked in the breath-taking view of the Atlantic Ocean as it stretched out before her. Listening to the happy babbling of the children in the backseat, she allowed it to soothe her further. It was most likely she had imagined seeing JJ across the road from her house and was allowing it to alarm her needlessly.

Taking a deep, cleansing breath of sea air, she decided to let it go and focus on enjoying their outing. She found the coastal road to Hout Bay intimidating and was grateful to have Adam at the wheel. Regardless of how daunting she might find the rugged coastline though, there was no denying the beauty that lay before her as the sun sparkled off the water.

While Hout Bay had been established as early as 1670, it wasn't until 1800 that the first house was built. It had been a popular area for felling trees to service the boat building industry, and eventually, it had grown into a fishing village to support the local community of farmers and labourers. It's popularity as a favourite seafood destination was still a major tourist attraction, and Willow's mouth watered just thinking about it.

Paying attention to the conversation flowing around her, she heard Adam pointing out sights to the girls and making funny comments about it to keep them interested and entertained. Adam singing a particularly bad ditty about shipwrecks and pirates inspired by the doomed oil tanker *MV Antipolis*, laying off the Oudekraal Beach, had the three girls dissolving in giggles. It certainly didn't prevent them from yelling "Aye, aye, Captain" when prompted and was cause for much hilarity.

Catching sight of Kelly out of the corner of her eye, Willow turned to look at her daughter. Willow saw a raw look of longing on the child's face as she looked at Adam. It hit her like a freight train in the chest. Until that point, she'd never considered that the children might miss having a father around. It had never once actually crossed her mind.

She'd been so busy trying to survive on her own and protect them from their biological father that she'd not stopped to consider that they might be missing the influence of a man. How had she missed something so integral to her daughters' lives? It floored her that she'd been so blind.

Willow saw Adam look at her briefly before turning his eyes back to the road.

Quietly, so only she'd hear him, he asked, "Okay there, honey? You've been very quiet this morning."

"I'm fine, thanks. I needed a few minutes to pull myself together. But it's all good now."

Reaching over, he gave her knee a gentle squeeze.

"Let me know if you need anything."

"I appreciate it, Adam, thanks. But really, I'm better now."

There was no way she was sharing her most recent, startling discovery. No way was she sharing that Kelly was eyeing him up as a potential dad, and Mommy wouldn't mind one bit.

"So where are we going?"

Allowing the topic change with no argument, Adam replied, "I thought we could take the three little madams to the beach and then have lunch at Seafarer's Landing in the harbour. They have the best sole ever."

"Sounds good, doesn't it, ladies?"

A trio of yeses rang out from the back of the car, their excitement palpable. Arriving in the small parking bay at Hout Bay harbour, the two adults helped the little ones out of the car, and they all made their way to the beach. The girls ran ahead to where water and sand met, squealing as the cold sea water washed over their tiny feet.

They splashed around, getting soaking wet. It was a good thing Willow was still in the habit of carrying extra clothing around for Chelsea and Kelly. They wouldn't dry in time for lunch and would be most uncomfortable having to sit at the table soaking wet. Adam, of course, had come prepared since he'd known where they were going.

Enjoying each other's company, the time flew by, and before they knew it, it was time for lunch. Willow and Adam worked as a team to get their children dried and dressed before heading over to the restaurant at the edge of the parking bay. The Seafarer's Landing was an institution in Hout Bay, popular with tourists and locals alike. The thirty-odd-year-old eatery was always full. Thankfully, Adam had clearly thought ahead and made sure to book a table.

Lunch over, they drove back into Cape Town, heading for the V and A Waterfront, which was a hive of activity. People milled around, making the most of their Sunday. Monday would arrive soon enough, but for now, they were determined to wring as much pleasure from the day as possible. The weather gods were smiling down on them. It was sunny and mild, as Cape Town showed herself to her best advantage.

Adam had planned a thoughtful list of girly activities, and Willow was suitably impressed. Among them was a visit to the semi-precious stone scratch patch, seal spotting, a train ride to the toy store, and lastly, each child got to pick a toy before ending the day with ice cream.

By the time they arrived at the ice cream store, the three pre-schoolers were starting to droop. It had been a long day filled with excitement and activity. Willow was so proud of Gracie and the twins. They'd been incredibly good, and their little group had received a number of admiring glances. At one point while at the restaurant, a lovely older lady had complimented them on being a beautiful family with such well-behaved children.

Willow had basked in the praise, indulging in a momentary daydream about what it would be like if they were, indeed, a family. Then she remembered the look on Kelly's face earlier, promptly snapping herself out of it. Right now, there was no telling where this would go, and she didn't want to create false hope for herself or her daughters only to have it shattered later.

She and Adam were still circling each other, and there was no telling where this was headed. Yes, she liked him as a person, a man, and she most certainly lusted after that glorious body of his, but she wasn't willing to leap before looking. She had to think of those two small children first. It wasn't only about her now. It hadn't been in years. She needed to take things slowly.

When they got home, Adam helped Willow get the girls ready for bed. They were utterly exhausted and started to whine, not wanting to eat or bathe before getting into bed. Standing firm about at least having a quick wash, Willow got them cleaned up in short order and into bed. Gracie was cuddled up with Chelsea in her bed since Adam had agreed to stay for dinner with Willow.

"Mommy, can Uncle Adam please read us a bedtime story? Please, Mommy, please?" Kelly asked.

Chelsea and Gracie added their voices to the request, and Adam was summoned to the bedroom.

"Rumour has it that my amazing reading skills are being sought, m'ladies. Is this so?"

"You're so funny, Daddy," Gracie chortled. "And you're speaking funny too."

"Uncle Adam is so funny," echoed Chelsea.

Adam gave one of his heart-stopping smiles, and Willow wanted to fan herself. Suddenly, the room seemed a few degrees warmer. Or maybe that was just her. Finally settling on a rather dog-eared copy of *Through the Looking Glass*, Chelsea handed it to Adam. Sitting in the rocking chair between the two beds, he began to read.

Willow sat at the foot of Kelly's bed, as Gracie was in Chelsea's. Popping a thumb in her mouth, a habit from babyhood, Kelly curled up tight against Willow, laying her head in her mother's lap. It wasn't long before Adam had all four of them completely entranced. Was there anything the man couldn't do well? He did all the voices, changing back and forth between characters without missing a beat.

He was so good that all three girls succumbed to sleep in a fairly short time.

"Adam," Willow called softly, so as not to wake anyone.

Looking up, Adam noticed Kelly curled up against Willow fast asleep. He placed the book on the nearest bedside table and stood to help move the child. Making sure each little girl was tucked up and comfortable, they kissed the girls and left the room quietly.

Heading for the kitchen, Willow turned to Adam to ask his preference for dinner. The look on Adam's face stopped her short.

"Is something wrong?"

Without a word, Adam reached for her, wrapping her up in an embrace before moving in for a kiss. A brain-frying, bone-melting kiss the likes of which Willow had never experienced. All thought ceased, and feeling sparked to life. Sinking into the embrace, Willow absorbed the taste and feel of Adam beneath her hands and lips.

Despite not knowing him very long, her body already recognised the smell of Adam. A combination of some mouth-watering aftershave, soap, and a warm, masculine scent unique to him. Her body recognised it and responded to it. It fired her senses and her hormones, making her want to taste him. All over.

CHAPTER ELEVEN

Adam didn't think he could last another minute without kissing Willow. He'd spent the entire day with her, watching her interact with her children and his own. It had touched him deeply, in a place he'd long ago locked away from the world, to watch how she had treated his daughter no different than her own.

When hugs, kisses, and cuddles were demanded, they were generously dished out to all three girls, and he'd watched his little girl blossom under the attention. He knew Gracie needed a woman's touch in her life, but he hadn't been willing to risk his badly battered heart to provide her with one.

But seeing how the child had opened like a flower

to the early morning sun, he realised he was short-changing her. He fully understood how his daughter felt. When Willow turned those deep sapphire eyes on him, he couldn't help but feel special. It made him feel like he was the only important thing in her world and what he had to say mattered.

It hit him in the solar plexus every time. Every. Single. Time. And, if he were frank, it hit him lower too. Much farther south. He couldn't remember a time he'd ever wanted a woman like he wanted her. He was beginning to think he hadn't even felt this way about Trisha despite thinking at the time that she was *the one*. Now he realised how wrong he'd been. She hadn't been, and he suspected she'd known that in some intuitive way.

Feeling Willow's response to his kiss had his pulse rising. Right along with his dick. God, he wanted this woman in the worst way. He could lose himself in her. It scared him how much he wanted to. She tasted of passion and heat. She felt like heaven under his hands. Made him long to run his fingertips over her naked skin, to taste the satiny softness of her.

Breaking the kiss, Adam rested his forehead on top of Willow's head. He breathed deeply, trying to calm his raging hormones. He certainly didn't want the first time he had her to be standing up in the middle of the passage. He started to speak, but passion had roughened his voice. Clearing his throat, he tried again.

"Honey, we have a choice here. Either we slow this thing down and grab that bite to eat, or we find somewhere a whole lot more comfortable than this passage. What's it going to be?"

Adam didn't want her to feel like he was railroading her into anything. If this was going to happen, it had to come from Willow. His erection straining at the zipper of his jeans, he prayed she wasn't about to suggest toasted sandwiches and coffee on the patio.

He wasn't sure he would survive it. When he was around her, he seemed to be in a permanent state of arousal. That was the potent effect she had on him.

Without a word, Willow took his hand and led him back in the direction they'd just come from. At the end of the passage, she turned left into a darkened room. She reached out a hand to turn the light on before moving farther into the room. Adam followed her. Willow came to a standstill in the middle of what was unmistakably a woman's bedroom. Elegant but inviting, just like the woman herself.

Unmoving, she waited, seemingly unsure now that they were standing in her space. Reaching out a hand, Adam gently ran the back of his fingers down Willow's cheek, marvelling at the softness of her skin. She was quite possibly the most beautiful woman he had ever met, both inside and out. And he couldn't believe she'd chosen to be with him.

Turning his hand over, he continued to trace

the contours of her face. Cupping her cheek for a moment, he stared into the ocean-deep beauty of her blue eyes, then allowed his hand to drop to her throat. Lightly, he wrapped his hand around her delicate neck, watching her eyes all the while to gauge her response. There were so many things he wanted to do with her, to her, but was unsure how receptive she'd be to it all.

At night, alone in his bed, his imagination tortured him as he saw his fantasies play out in his mind like a showing of his own personal late-night movie. Seeing her splayed out on his bed, bound and blindfolded, awaiting his pleasure. Although he didn't live the lifestyle, he'd dreamed about finding the right woman to try it with. Willow pushed all the right buttons for him.

He just wasn't sure if tonight was the right time to chance it. This was their first time together, and he didn't want to ruin it before it had even begun.

Hearing her swiftly indrawn breath, he felt himself tighten as he watched her eyes begin to glaze and her cheeks flush a gentle pink as passion took hold. God, this woman was so responsive. He'd barely touched her, and she was already coming to life.

Coming to a decision, Adam moulded her soft curves to his harder frame. Leaning into her, eyes holding hers, he lowered his head until his lips barely touched hers.

"Do you trust me, Willow?"

Trepidation evident on her face, she slowly nodded.

Giving her bottom lip a nip, he soothed it with a sensual slide of his tongue.

"Will you trust me now, Willow?"

Again, she nodded. Hesitantly. The tension in the room ratcheted up.

"Where do you keep your scarves?"

Wordlessly, she went over to a chest of drawers

against a wall. Adam followed her over, looking at the contents of the drawer. Spotting a scarf that looked soft, he reached in to touch it. Pulling the soft material out, he slid the drawer closed.

Stepping back from her, Adam ran the scarf through his fingers, continuing to hold her gaze steadily while trying to decide whether he wanted to blindfold her or bind her with it.

"Undress for me, Willow."

Her tongue darted out to wet her now dry lips. He saw how nervous the situation seemed to be making her as she turned away, her hands reaching up to undo the buttons on the front of her blouse.

"No, Willow."

She turned her head as Adam's voice stopped her.

"I told you to undress for me. Not to just get undressed. Turn around. I want to watch you undress for me. Do it slowly."

Watching her still, he waited patiently to see how

she would react.

Willow's eyes widened at this new Adam. She'd always found him to be confident and assertive, but suddenly, he seemed so much more . . . More what? Dominant? Commanding? Demanding? It didn't really matter to her at that moment. She just felt something inside her respond. Her core heated, and her panties dampened. Oh, so slowly, she began to undo the buttons on her blouse, letting the two halves fall open as she went, allowing Adam to glimpse the lacy red bra she wore beneath.

She watched as his lips parted. He drew a breath in and knew she wasn't the only one feeling that something special that seemed to be humming in the air around them. Undoing the last button, she allowed the blouse to glide down her arms and fall to the floor. Reaching for the zipper of her jeans, she pulled it down equally slow. Shimmying it over her hips, she ran her hands down her leg, dragging the material down too. Eventually, she stood in just her bra and matching lacy boy shorts.

The heat in Adam's eyes flared as he took her in, standing there in nothing more than a couple scraps of lace. Circling her, he reached up and released the clip that held her hair. The heavy curtain of silken curls cascaded down her back, nearly reaching to her gloriously rounded ass. Fisting a gentle hand in the waves, he drew her head backwards and held her gaze.

"Do you trust me?" Adam asked softly.

Willow nodded, wordlessly.

"I'd like to blindfold you. Are you willing to try that with me?"

She hesitated a long moment before nodding again, her gaze dropping away from his.

"Willow, look at me."

Slowly she lifted her gaze back to his. Reaching

out a gentle hand, he cradled her cheek. She took in a deep breath. Just that simple touch helped ease some of her nervousness.

"If you're uncomfortable with where I'm taking this, you need to tell me, honey. I want to hear the words."

Not knowing what to expect, Willow wasn't sure quite how she felt, but she was willing to try it. At the very least, she did trust Adam not to hurt her.

"I'm not sure if comfortable is the right word, but I'm willing to try this with you."

She could see how her words affected Adam in the way he first swallowed and then smiled at her. That smile of his should come with a warning. It was absolutely lethal. Closing her eyes, she tilted her head slightly to make it easier for him to see what he was doing and waited. She didn't have long to wait. Adam placed the scarf over her eyes, tying it firmly but gently.

"Okay? Not too tight?"

Breathing through the nervousness, Willow shook her head.

"No, it's not too tight."

"Can you see anything past the blindfold?"

"No, nothing. It's quite dark."

Cupping her chin, Adam rubbed a thumb over her full bottom lip.

"That's good. You're meant to feel only, not see. But Willow, I need you to understand that you can call a stop to things anytime. If there's anything that makes you uncomfortable or if you don't like something, I need you to tell me. Just one word and it all comes to an end. All you have to do is say stop. No fancy words or gimmicks. Just simply stop. Yes?"

"Yes."

She licked her lips nervously again. Taking her hands, Adam led Willow over to her bed. He lowered her gently to the mattress and ordered her to lie back.

She scooted back, stretching out as instructed. She heard the rustle of clothing and could only deduce that Adam was getting undressed. Disappointment washed over her. Watching him undress was something she'd been looking forward to.

Not expecting it, Willow jumped as she felt a soft touch on the sole of her foot. Just the lightest touch. Relaxing into it, she felt the sensation moving up her foot and over the top. Slowly, slowly, that gentlest of touches continued up her calf, moving ever closer to the juncture of her thighs. Suddenly, the disappointment of not seeing him undress for her wasn't quite so important.

Her skin tingled wherever Adam touched her, and she felt herself going slick in anticipation of his touch at her very core. She moved restlessly under his hand, trying to encourage him to go faster. To touch her where it ached. Adam merely placed the softest of kisses on her mound before removing her panties.

Willow mewled in protest. He was winding her tighter and tighter, and she wasn't sure how much longer she'd be able to hold out before she combusted. He soothed her with butterfly kisses across her abdomen, his hand heading ever upwards. When Adam enclosed her hardened nipple in the warm, wet cavern of his mouth, she was not expecting it. She was so focused on the glide of his hand across her skin, she'd become accustomed to his dodge and pass tactics, it caught her completely unaware. Her torso left the bed in response to the deep pulling that echoed all the way in her core. He used the lace trapped between his tongue and the pebbled nub to create a different kind of friction.

No longer able to hold her silence, Willow whispered into the dark void.

"Adam, please. I need . . ."

"Tell me. What do you need?"

She wasn't sure what she needed; she just knew

she needed something to soothe the burn he was building so skilfully inside her. Her skin felt hot and too tight. Her clit begged for attention.

"I need…," she tried again.

"Shh, it's okay. I'll take care of you, honey. I promise."

Reaching around her, Adam undid the clasp of her bra and removed it before returning his attention to the nipple he'd been lavishing attention on, pulling it back into his mouth. Willow's legs rubbed restlessly against each other. Lost in the dark that encapsulated her world behind the blindfold, she felt every little touch. Every electrifying little touch.

While Adam's mouth worked magic at her breast, she felt his hand begin to knead her thigh, moving higher with each stroke, until she felt the back of his fingers brush against her clit. The touch caused her to cry out. *Yes! That!* That was what she needed. She needed him to touch her, to soothe the almost unbearable ache. She couldn't remember a time that she ever *needed* quite like this. With this intensity. Although, right this minute, she didn't remember much of anything. Being unable to see what Adam was doing, all Willow could do was feel.

The firm pressure of Adam's thumb on her fully engorged clit had Willow arching off the bed again.

"Oh God, Adam!"

She was drowning in pleasure. Adrift. She needed his touch to anchor her, just as she needed it to send her over the edge. Between the pull of his mouth and the friction of his very talented thumb, Willow felt herself start to unravel. But it was when he worked two fingers into her tight, wet channel she came apart spectacularly for him. Her body bowed up. The muscles of her centre clamped down on Adam's fingers like a clenched fist. She couldn't contain her cry of pleasure. It was almost as if it was ripped from her very depths.

So intense was the ecstasy she barely noticed that Adam had removed his fingers until she felt the head of his cock nudge her drenched opening. She hadn't even noticed he'd donned a condom. He groaned, long and low, as he eased into her. For a second, she tensed as she felt the size of him stretch her, working muscles that hadn't been worked in too long, making them burn as he stretched her with his girth. The moment of discomfort passed quickly as her body adjusted to accommodate him.

Adam paused to savour the sensation of being balls-deep in heaven. It had been so long that he needed a minute to catch his breath and just absorb the feel of her beneath him. Levering himself up on his arms, he looked down at the glorious sight before him. Willow spread out on the bed, a golden halo of hair cascading over the pillow, trapping her as she lay on it. All her lush curves laid open to him.

He ran his tongue over a tightly furled nipple before blowing a stream of air over the wet tip. In fascination, he watched as it tightened ever further. Adam adored how responsive Willow was and that she wasn't afraid to show it. She participated wholeheartedly, holding nothing of herself back.

His body clamouring for more, Adam began to move. God, she felt so good wrapped around him, tight and hot. Willow began to move with him, and they soon found their rhythm. He could hear the sounds of sex as he thrust into her over and over again. The tension growing until he felt his balls draw up close to his body.

Keeping the pace up, he felt Willow go even slicker around him, the walls of her channel rippling, warning him of her impending orgasm. He quickened his pace and prayed he could last. It had been a while for him, and, to be honest, he was surprised he hadn't gone off like the fourth of July already.

Willow cried out and clamped down on him, dragging him over the edge with her. Adam was sure the top of his head was going to come off. He couldn't remember ever coming this hard. Lowering himself to his elbows, he removed Willow's blindfold.

She was lying with her eyes closed, trying to catch her breath. He stared down at her, his thoughts churning. She'd been magnificent. Responsive and giving. The best sex he'd had, hands down. It made him feel things that he didn't want to feel. It made him feel, period. It scared the bejesus out of him.

He didn't want his heart involved. He'd survived Trisha leaving him because he'd had to. He'd been all that Gracie had left. He was beginning to suspect that maybe it had been more his ego that had taken the beating than his heart, but that didn't mean he wanted to chance having it stomped on again, just in case. But he didn't want to be a dick to Willow either. She didn't deserve that.

Smoothing the hair back from her face, Adam dropped a quick kiss on her forehead before pulling out of her and rolling to the edge of the bed. He heard Willow move and turned to see her looking at him. Her gaze still slightly unfocused.

"Hi there," was all he could manage.

"Hi yourself."

"I'll be back in a sec, honey. I just need to get rid of this." Adam pointed at the condom as he rose from the bed and quickly headed for the *en suite* bathroom, closing the door behind him.

Willow felt like she was experiencing an out of body moment. Damn, that man knew how to make a woman feel special. When Adam removed the blindfold, she wanted to protest. She'd not done anything like that before but would be quite happy to do it again. It was simply amazing. Having to rely on feeling every sensation had been incredible.

Everything felt so much more intense, and she'd loved every minute of it.

Initially, she'd been nervous, not knowing what to expect. But Adam had been so gentle with her, making the experience earth-shatteringly good. But now that the blindfold was gone and she could see again, he seemed a bit off somehow. Willow was sure it wasn't her imagination. When he'd gotten up to use the bathroom, he'd had a strange look on his face.

Some of the joy of the moment drained away as she realised that maybe the experience hadn't been as good for Adam as it had been for her. She really hoped she hadn't done anything to spoil it for him. She was feeling a bit emotionally raw after their mind-blowing sex, and it made her want to cry. *Pull yourself together, Willow. What's the matter with you?*

She took a deep, calming breath when she heard the bathroom door open, turning to smile at Adam as he came towards her. He walked past her to where his clothes lay in a heap on the floor and picked his boxer briefs up. Pulling them on he came to sit on the side of the bed.

Willow steeled herself. Reaching out a hand, he ran his fingers through her hair as it lay on the pillow.

"You doing all right, honey? I didn't hurt you? Scare you?"

"No. I'm good, Adam. That was . . . Wow."

He smiled at her words, but his heart didn't seem to be in it, and hers beat a little harder. *Oh God, he's going to give me the brush-off. He's gotten what he wanted, and now he's going to tell me goodbye.* Willow's thoughts tumbled over each other in misery. When would she learn men couldn't be trusted? She'd thought he was different.

"I have to get going. I have the day shift tomorrow, so it's an early start for me."

Blinking to keep the tears at bay, she nodded.

"No problem. Let me just get my robe, and I'll

let you out."

Rolling away from Adam so he wouldn't see the tears she hadn't managed to beat back, Willow got off on the other side of the bed. She collected her robe from the back of the bathroom door and stood with her back to Adam as she pulled it on, feeling like a fool.

She hadn't heard him move, but she suddenly felt his body heat against her back. *How did such a big man move so quietly?* She wondered. Wrapping his arms around her from behind, she felt his lips on her temple.

"That was incredible. Thank you for letting me share that with you."

"It *was* incredible," Willow echoed, not knowing what else to say. Suddenly, the easy rapport they'd shared all weekend had evaporated.

She actually couldn't wait to get him out the door so she could be alone. She just couldn't figure out what had gone wrong. Maybe when what they were feeling was a little less new, a little less raw – whatever it may be — she could ask him what had changed. For now, she absorbed the feel of him surrounding her before leading him to the girls' room so he could collect his daughter.

Willow stood by the door watching him buckle a still unconscious Gracie into her car seat. Adam closed the door and headed back her way. He stopped in front of her and pulled her into his arms. He kissed her, slow and tender, which seemed at odds with how he'd been behaving since they'd made love.

Lifting his head, he placed another kiss on her forehead before stepping back.

"I have to go, but I'll give you a call tomorrow. Go on in and lock up. I'll wait."

"Okay. Night, Adam. Chat to you tomorrow."

"Night, honey."

Willow locked up and went to stand at her living

room window to let Adam know she was all safely locked up. He waved to her as he headed for his car in her driveway. She watched as he climbed into the SUV. Once he'd pulled away from the house, Willow let the curtain fall, heading for her bedroom with a heavy heart.

Adam cursed himself all the way home. He managed to get quite creative with the names he called himself on the ten-minute drive. He'd had what was, quite possibly, the singularly most spectacular connection with another human being in all his life, and he'd spoiled it by behaving like a prize dick. He'd seen the hurt in Willow's eyes, even though she hadn't said a word.

It was not his finest moment. What had started out as nothing more than sex for him had taken a turn towards an emotional connection somewhere along the way. He'd panicked. And he'd hurt her.

Stopping his SUV in front of his garage, he hit the remote to open the door. He dropped his head onto the steering wheel in front of him. Pushing a hard breath out through his mouth, Adam tried to get a grip on his thoughts.

He needed to figure this thing out. Then tomorrow, he needed to find a way to apologise to Willow. To make it up to her. She didn't deserve the way he'd treated her tonight. But before he contacted Willow, he'd phone his mom. She was just the person to help him figure this out. He didn't think something as clichéd as flowers was going to do the trick in this situation. Whatever the solution, he needed to make this right.

Five thirty. That's what her cell phone said. Willow finally admitted defeat and got up. It had been a crappy night. She'd tossed and turned all night trying to quiet her thoughts long enough to get some sleep but had little success.

Five thirty was still pretty dark out, but she felt a strong need to sit out on her patio and soak up the silence and the beauty around her. She needed it to soothe the ragged edges of her emotions. If she could only figure out where she'd messed up, then maybe she could figure out how to fix it.

After a magical weekend spending time with Adam and Gracie, feeling what it could be like to be a family, to have a man around you could trust, Willow felt raw. Adam's hasty departure the night before had left her reeling, trying to understand what she'd done wrong. Had she said or done something wrong?

If her mother was to be believed, she was the reason her father had left. She had never understood how she'd caused him to leave, but maybe that was the problem. She hadn't figured it out, so maybe she was repeating the pattern. Or maybe she was simply unlovable.

Pulling on her robe and some socks to keep her warm, Willow headed for the kitchen. She needed coffee if she had any chance of functioning at all today. As she made her way down the passage, she thought she heard a noise at the front door. Standing still, she listened. Not hearing it again, she decided her overtired brain was playing tricks on her. Coffee was definitely required.

Mug in hand, Willow curled her legs under her as she watched the rest of the world sleeping around her. The twins would be waking soon, but for the moment, she had time to breathe in the peace and tranquillity surrounding her like a comforting hug. A soothing balm to her flagging spirits. If she was going to fix this thing with Adam, she needed to work out where she'd gone wrong, but for now, she just needed to be.

CHAPTER TWELVE

"Dude, you look like crap. What the hell did you do on your weekend off that's left you looking like a limp dishrag?"

Gavin's booming voice rang out through the office, causing some of the other officers to look his way.

"Wanna take a front page out there, bud? Maybe a spot on the radio? I don't think enough people heard you."

"Oooh, grumpy too. It must have been a doozy."

Not even bothering to answer his partner, Adam simply showed him the middle finger. Laughing, Gavin walked over to his desk. Shrugging out of his jacket, he hung the garment over the back of his chair before settling his six-foot-five frame onto the protesting seat.

"One of these days, that thing's going to give it up, and you're going to land in a heap on the floor. You know I'm going to laugh at you first before I help you up, right?"

Grinning, Gavin replied, "Me and this chair go way back. She'll hold me."

"If you say so."

"Wanna talk about it? I can see something's eating at you, bud."

Looking at his friend, Adam contemplated talking it over with him. Finally, he shook his head.

"Thanks, Gav, maybe another time. I appreciate the offer though."

Gavin studied him for a heartbeat too long, making Adam uncomfortable. He imagined his friend was seeing far more than he wanted him to.

"Any time. You know where to find me when you're ready."

He nodded. That reminded him, he wanted to talk to his mom.

"I have to head out for a few minutes. I won't be long."

"Sure. Take your time. I've got it covered."

Adam pulled his sports jacket on, heading for the door. Rather than phone his mom, he'd pop in to see her. He hadn't seen her or his dad in a while. Stopping at the mall up the road from his office, he got his mom a bunch of her favourite flowers.

Pulling into the drive, Adam sat and looked at his childhood home. It brought back so many happy memories. Love and laughter had echoed through the rooms, wrapping those who dwelled within those walls in the security that they were cherished. He and his brothers knew, without a doubt, they were deeply loved and always welcome.

But sitting in his car, reminiscing all day wasn't going to get him anywhere. Grabbing the flowers off the passenger seat, he got out and headed for the front door.

Letting himself in with his key, Adam called out, "Mom, you home?"

Hearing voices coming from the kitchen, he made his way down the passage to what his mother considered the heart of her home. As a stay-at-home mom, that's where she could be found, more often than not, when they were living at home. There was always something mouth-watering to eat when they got back from school and, later, college.

"Adam!" his mom greeted him, getting to her feet. "I didn't hear you come in. How are you, my boy?"

Adam enfolded his mom in a hug, inhaling the familiar scent of her perfume. He felt an ache in the region of his heart. Without another word, as if she knew he needed it, his mother held him a little tighter. After a long moment, he gentled his hold, dropping a kiss on the top of his mom's head.

"Adam. We weren't expecting you," his dad spoke from behind him.

"Hey, Pop. I needed some motherly advice, so I thought I'd swing by for a quick cuppa."

He went over and shook his father's extended hand.

"It's always good to see you, son. Come, sit. Violet, the boy needs one of your cuppas, my love." Turning back to Adam, he continued, "Looks like you're carrying the burden of the world on your shoulders there, my boy. Let's have that cup of coffee. Then you can tell your mother what ails you while I go sweep the paving."

"Thanks, Dad. Appreciate it."

"Here you go. Careful, it's hot."

Smiling his thanks, Adam took a seat at the

kitchen table. He chatted about this and that with his parents as they all drank their coffee, catching up on each other's lives. Draining his mug, Adam's father got up, taking his mug over to the kitchen sink. He rinsed the mug and left it to drain as he made his way out of the kitchen.

"Catch you later, kid," he called back over his shoulder.

"Later, Pop."

His mother snagged his attention by laying a gentle hand over one of his.

"What's got you in such a tizzy, my sweet boy?"

Resting his other hand on top of his mother's, Adam rested his forehead there for a moment as he gathered his thoughts, drawing comfort from the familiarity of that soothing touch. This was hard for him, but he really needed to make things right with Willow. He'd been such a dick the night before. And no one gave good advice like his mom.

"I've met someone, Mom."

"Ah," was all his mother said, giving him a much-too-knowing look. Her amber eyes, so much like his own, were shrewd in their assessment. It felt almost like his mother could see all the way into his soul. "Tell me about her."

Adam looked at his watch. He was on official time, and his captain would have his bullocks for breakfast if he knew he was having a hearts-and-flowers talk with his "Mommy" while on duty, but he knew he wouldn't be able to concentrate if he didn't resolve this now. And he sure as hell wasn't doing this over the phone, especially not at the office. He could just imagine what a good laugh the guys would have at his expense. He'd never live it down, that was for sure.

"God, Mom, I don't even know where to start. All I know is I've messed up big time, and I don't know how to fix it. You're the only one I can trust to give me solid advice."

"It's always best to start at the beginning. How did you meet this– I take it we're talking about a lady here?"

Barking out a surprised laugh at the unexpected question, Adam shook his head.

"Geez. I didn't see that one coming. Of course it's a woman, Mom."

"So, tell me how you met this young lady?"

Adam started to talk. And once he started, the words poured out. He'd had no idea he could talk so much at one time. He didn't think he ever had. He definitely hadn't realised he had so much to say about Willow. Eventually, the words slowed then stopped. Sitting back in his chair he eyed the remnants of his coffee that had gone cold, unnoticed in his hand.

Suddenly feeling embarrassed to have said so much, such personal things, to his mother, he got up to rinse his mug. He placed it on the drying rack next to his father's cup but remained standing with his back to the older woman.

"What do I do, Mom?"

"Come sit. Let's see what we can do to make things right with your young lady."

His mom spoke, he listened. He paid attention to the wisdom of many years of happy marriage. The older couple had recently celebrated their forty-fifth wedding anniversary, so he figured if anybody knew what they were talking about, it would be his parents.

Hearing the beep of a message, Adam took his phone out of the pocket of his jeans. He saw the time on the display as he went to read the message.

"Shit, I've got to go, Mom. I'll call you later."

As Violet stood to see her son out, he gave her a hug, holding on like she was his anchor in rough seas. Maybe she was since he felt so out of his depth right then. Hugging him back tight, they stood there like that for a long moment.

"You'd best be on your way, baby. Don't want you getting into trouble."

They made their way out to the front of the house, Adam stopping to say goodbye to his father. They spoke a few words before he headed for his car. He really needed to get going. Before climbing behind the wheel, Adam turned to his parents, taking in the older couple standing with their arms around each other, looking like all was right in the world. He guessed in their world it probably was.

"Thank you, Mom. For everything."

A soft smile lit Violet's face.

"Anytime, my boy."

Lifting a hand in farewell, he got into his car. Driving away from his childhood home, he looked back and saw his parents standing on the curb, arms still around each other. They'd been his example of a good, solid marriage. He'd thought that's what he had with Trisha until he'd wised up to the fact that the only important person in Trisha's life was Trisha.

For the first time since his marriage had ended, Adam was willing to give it another go. He just had to convince Willow he wasn't a complete jackass. He needed to get back to the office and get his head back in the game. Making it up to Willow for his poor behaviour the night before would have to wait for the moment.

Another Monday almost over, Willow sighed in relief. She had a tension headache and couldn't wait to get home. She'd considered staying home for the day but in the end, had come to work. Wallowing in misery at home would have been unbearable. So here she was.

She hadn't heard a word from Adam all day. Recently, they'd been in touch at least once a day. Today, he'd been ominously quiet. Willow just wished there was someone she could talk to. The only person she would even consider talking to was thousands of miles away, the time difference making her day his night. If she worked it out right, she could maybe call Brett when it was morning for him.

Her brother was the only person she had left that she could turn to. Long ago, she'd accepted that her mother hated her. She blamed Willow for the breakdown of her marriage instead of seeing her husband as the shallow, weak, and selfish man he was. They'd never been close.

Brett had always protected her from her mother, as best a young boy could. He'd been the one she'd turned to for everything. As they got older, he'd gotten more protective of her. But eventually, he'd left her too. Oh, she got it that he had to live his own life, that he couldn't put his life on hold to shield her from their mother forever. But that didn't mean it didn't hurt like hell when he moved half a world away. And no matter what she told herself, she couldn't help but feel he'd abandoned her too.

She missed him like crazy, wishing he were there now. She needed his common-sense advice and no-nonsense outlook on life. In the deep recesses of her mind, Willow realised that she was quite possibly blowing this thing with Adam way out of proportion, but it pushed every hot button around her feelings of self-worth.

Surely, if the man who was partially responsible for her existence couldn't be bothered to stick around, then didn't that say something about her? Huffing out a frustrated breath, she dropped her head onto the desk. She was sick of these thoughts that circled in her mind with no answer.

Maybe she *should* video call Brett. It would help her put this in perspective. Help her find peace of mind. Or maybe she should scrape her courage together and go directly to the source of her mental anguish. At least if she hashed this out with Adam, she would know where she stood.

Sitting up, she squared her shoulders. That's what she'd do. She would talk to Adam about last night. She would still call Brett. She really needed to connect with him. It had been a while since they'd last chatted anyway, so it was time for a catch-up session. Before her courage deserted her, she grabbed her phone to text Adam. She wasn't quite brave enough to phone him yet.

Willow: Hi. Was wondering if you've got time to pop in this evening? W

Feeling a little more settled within herself for having taken a proactive step, Willow turned her attention back to the admin that she'd been trying to do all day. It wasn't long when her cell phone beeped, indicating she had a message. Picking it up, she saw it was Adam. That was quicker than anticipated.

Adam: Sure. What time works for you?

Willow: How about 7?

Adam: 7's good. See you then.

Willow blew out a sigh. A sick feeling settled in her stomach, but she really needed to know why Adam was blowing hot and cold suddenly.

Willow's heart was beating uncomfortably. The closer it got to seven o'clock, the more she wondered if she'd done the wrong thing. Dealing with an issue head on had always been her style. A product of her upbringing. Her mother had always alluded to or intimated, hidden her emotions behind nasty actions. Very rarely had Monica come out and actually voiced the ugly accusations out loud.

Now that Adam was due to arrive any moment, she thought maybe it would have been better to let things lie for a couple more days. What was done was done. She wasn't about to chicken out now. She could do this. Besides, before getting in any deeper, she'd rather know the score upfront.

The mail she'd brought with her when they'd gotten home lay on the table. As she was about to reach for it, the doorbell rang. Her heart lurched, and the knot in her stomach tightened almost unbearably.

Checking the security peephole first, Willow saw a rather apprehensive-looking Adam standing there, holding Gracie's hand. Heart sinking even further, she opened the door.

"Willow, hey."

"Hey yourself."

She closed the door behind him before leading the way to the living room as Gracie dashed off down the hall to the girls' room.

"Have a seat. Can I get you anything to drink?"

"No thanks. I'm good."

Great! Right back to awkward. Not an encouraging start, but Willow wasn't backing down. They'd either get the air cleared, or things were going to get a whole lot more awkward. Either way, she needed it done. Now.

Curling up in her favourite seat, Willow examined Adam. He sat in the single chair, hands hanging between his spread knees as his elbows rested on them. If she didn't know any better, it was almost as if he was expecting her to give him marching orders.

She couldn't fathom how they'd gone from having a fabulous time together, a deeply intimate time, to being back to borderline strangers. Tonight's conversation would determine where this relationship was headed.

"I need—" Adam started.

"I don't—" Willow said at the same time.

They both stopped. Willow wanted to tell Adam to finish what he was going to say. *She* needed to know what *he* needed to say, but Adam beat her to it.

"Sorry. Go ahead."

Taking a moment to collect herself again, Willow

continued.

"Now that we're here, I don't quite know where to start. But if I had to pick a place, I'd say the thing that's weighing on me most is what happened yesterday. We had a wonderful day together. Then we had mind-blowing sex together. And then, suddenly, you couldn't get out the door quick enough." Willow paused a second to gather her composure. She'd promised herself she wouldn't get emotional – men hated that. But the tears gathered in her eyes regardless.

She couldn't deny his behaviour had hurt her. Shaking her head, Willow swallowed. The emotion rose up, choking her, and she couldn't get another word out. She sat staring at her hands as she tried to gather her composure.

Adam sighed. Looking up, she saw he was watching her with a pained expression on his handsome face.

"Willow . . ." Adam cleared his throat, looking miserable. "I'm sorry. I never meant to hurt you. Things got intense pretty quickly, and I wasn't prepared for where it went. That doesn't excuse my behaviour, but . . ."

Adam's cell phone rang. Swearing viciously, he reached into his pocket to grab the offending instrument. Seeing the number for dispatch displayed on the screen, he seriously contemplated hurling it across the room before looking over at Willow.

"Sorry, honey. Give me a second. I have to take this," he said to Willow before connecting the call. "Dawson."

He listened as the dispatcher spoke.

"Where's Jefferson or Clark?" he bit out, irritated. Listening again, he eventually replied. "Fine. I'll be there as soon as I can."

Willow rose to her feet in anticipation of seeing Adam to the door. She was actively beginning to hate his cell phone. It seemed to have a knack of ringing at all the wrong times. But it was his job, and there wasn't anything either of them could do about it. It was what it was.

Rising too, Adam walked over to where she stood. Cupping her cheeks gently in his large palms, he rested his forehead against hers and heaved a sigh.

"This didn't go according to plan. I'm so sorry, Willow. A riot has broken out in one of the informal settlements, and the calls are flooding in about assaults and killings. To top it off, we're apparently short staffed now due to a flu virus. I have to go. I don't want to, but I don't have a choice."

"It's okay, Adam. Really. I understand."

"I need to get Gracie to my folks." Lifting his head to look into her eyes, hoping she'd see the sincerity there, he continued, "This isn't over. We still need to talk."

"Yes, I agree. We do. In the meantime, you need

to get going. Leave Gracie here with us. It's not a problem. That way you don't have to worry your folks."

"That's very generous. Are you sure?"

"Of course. Besides, here she at least has someone her own age to keep her company. If you get done too late, she can stay over, and I'll drop her off along with the girls in the morning."

"Thank you. I appreciate it, honey." Turning to leave, Adam turned back, the pained expression back on his handsome face. "I know I was out of line leaving things like I did last night. I'm sorry."

Willow was silent for a moment as she studied him, seeing the sincerity of his apology reflected in the warm amber of his eyes. Nodding acceptance of his apology, she stepped towards him.

"We'll talk another time. You need to be on your way."

Adam looked as if he wanted to argue but

apparently decided to let it go.

Having said goodbye to his daughter, promising to phone Willow as soon as he got a chance, he walked to the front door. Standing in the doorway, she watched him walk away from her.

"Adam."

He stopped and turned back.

"Yeah?"

"Be safe, okay?"

A poor simile of his usual cocky grin flitted across his mouth.

"Always."

Turning on his heel one last time, he headed for his car.

Having watched until the headlights of his car disappeared, Willow finally headed back to the living room, frustrated at not having resolved the issue with Adam. Spying the neglected mail on the coffee table, she picked it up, curled up in her favourite spot and shuffled through trying to take her mind off the conversation they still needed to have and the fact that Adam's job was leading him smack-dab in the middle of danger for who knew how long.

Her heart rate kicked up when she spotted the white, hand printed envelope in the pile in her hand. Putting all the mail down on the sofa beside her, she went to fetch gloves and a Ziploc bag before opening the envelope. She read the message.

Time's up bitch.

Fear, metallic and unpleasant, washed through Willow. Stuffing the message and envelope into the Ziploc bag, she flung it away from her as if it had burned her. Unsure what to make of it but knowing it meant nothing good, she wasn't sure what to do next. Previously, she'd phoned Adam without even thinking about it. Now she was unsure. Besides, she didn't want to distract him when he was going into the heart of a violent riot.

Getting up to pace, Willow worried at her thumbnail while she considered her options. She didn't know how to get hold of Adam's partner, Gavin. It was pointless phoning her brother. And she knew the police station where Adam was stationed was short-staffed tonight, so it was pointless calling them too.

Coming to the conclusion Adam was probably the only person she *could* call, she went over to her phone. Picking it up, she paced around the room some more. She'd dialled and hung up numerous times as indecision plagued her. Eventually, she let the call connect. She listened to the phone ring and eventually go to voicemail, experiencing a moment of doubt. Did that mean he was just too busy to answer or had his apology not been as sincere as she'd taken it to be?

Taking a deep breath, she decided to give him the benefit of the doubt, leaving a message when prompted to do so.

"Hi, Adam. The girls are all fine. But could you please give me a call back as soon as you get this? Something's come up, and I really need to talk to you about it."

Following the voice prompt, she pushed the hash key before hanging up. All she could do now was wait for him to call back. She went back to pacing, worrying at her thumbnail once more.

CHAPTER THIRTEEN

The noise level was intense. The group of rioters shouted, chanted, sang, whistled, and stomped their feet as they danced their war dance. Bodies milled around the entrance to the township, looting and laying waste to anything in their path. The settlement, located in an outlying suburb of Cape Town, had been the site of many such events in the past.

Well-versed in dealing with this type of situation, Adam drove on the periphery of the group, looking for uniformed officers. He kept an eagle eye on the crowd, knowing they could turn on him at any second. Any and all were fair game when a group of rioters were this riled up.

Spotting a uniformed barricade up ahead, he eased his way towards it. When he reached the barrier, an officer stepped forward to stop him.

"Sir, you shouldn't be in the area. It's too dangerous for civilians at the moment."

"Evening, Officer." Adam greeted, flashing his police credentials. "I'm responding to dispatch's report of a murder near the taxi rank."

"Evening, sir," the uniform replied. "Yeah, I know which one you're speaking of. I'll send someone with you to show you where to go."

Turning, he called another officer over to show Adam to the crime scene.

"Stay sharp, sir. They're really agitated tonight."

"Gotcha. Thanks."

The crime scene wasn't too far from where they were but was thankfully substantially quieter than where he'd just come from. A trail of devastation lay before him, a silent testimony to the violence that had recently passed that way.

He parked his SUV where a couple of other police vehicles stood, their blue lights cutting harshly through the surrounding dark. Nearby, spotlights had been set up to provide light for police officials already on site. Adam spotted the covered body as a group of personnel parted to allow him to pass. He made his way over to it.

The officer who had guided him called to someone, and he turned to look. A tall man also in uniform jogged over to them.

"Serfontein," the officer called. "Can you please assist Detective Dawson? I need to get back to the barricade. Things are crazy back there."

"Sure. No problem," the man named Serfontein replied.

Adam thanked the departing officer before turning his attention to Constable Serfontein. The grim business of murder absorbed his attention as he got the rundown from the constable before starting with interviewing eye witnesses and getting as many statements as he could.

Hours after he'd gotten to the scene, Adam finally made his way tiredly back to his vehicle. He pulled his cell phone out of the front pocket of his jeans to check for messages. Scrolling through, he saw there was a missed call from Willow from hours earlier and a text message from her a few hours later.

He called his voicemail first.

"Hi, Adam. The girls are all fine. But could you please give me a call back as soon as you get this? Something's come up, and I really need to talk to you about it," he heard Willow say.

Looking at his watch, he saw it was already near quarter past one. He saved the message and exited voicemail to check her text message.

Willow: I'm sorry to bug you. I understand that you're busy, but I really do need to talk to you so I just wanted to let you know you can call me anytime, whatever time you get this message.

Unease prickled along Adam's scalp. Willow said the girls were okay. She didn't say she was. He looked out at the scene before him, trying to decide whether he should phone back now or leave it until the morning. On the one hand, it was late to be calling, but on the other hand, he wasn't sure he'd get much sleep worrying about Willow. It wasn't what she said that had him uneasy. It was more how she'd said it.

Whether she was aware of it or not, she had sounded scared in her voicemail. Deciding he would call her, he dialled her number and listened to it ring. He continued to look out over the crime scene while he waited.

Sitting in her brightly lit bedroom, Willow tried unsuccessfully to read her book. The romance novel was doing absolutely nothing to keep her distracted from her thoughts. As the hours dragged by, she found it increasingly difficult to curb her fear.

The note she'd received lay on her dressing table like a dark omen of things to come. As she swung her legs over the side of her bed to go look at the note, yet again, her cell phone rang. Seeing it was Adam, she said a silent prayer of thanks and answered the call.

"Hi, Adam."

"I'm sorry to only call back now. I never heard my phone ring while I was busy processing the scene. I only saw your messages when I got back to the car. Are you okay?"

Hearing a noise at the front of the house, Willow got up, intending to investigate the noise she'd heard.

"Not really, no. I got another one of those notes again. That's why I called you. But now I hear a noise at the front of the house."

"Go to the girls and lock yourself up in the room, if you can. I'll ask one of the vans on patrol to swing past the house while I make my way back to you."

She continued down the passage as they spoke.

"No, I'll just have a quick–" The door burst open, triggering the silent alarm. Willow screamed.

Looking at JJ standing on her doorstep, her blood ran cold

"What the hell are you doing here?" she cried out.

Adam was yelling at her on the phone, but she was so focused on the man standing in front of her she didn't hear him. She stood with the phone in her hand, frozen in shock.

The sound of flesh connecting with flesh, as he landed a vicious blow, sounded harsh in the quiet night.

"Shut up," he screamed at her. "I told you time was up, bitch. I want what's mine."

Suddenly fearing what he'd do to the children, Willow swung around, intending to run to the girls' room and lock herself in with them, to keep them safe from the monster that was their father. She should have listened to Adam.

JJ grabbed a fist-full of her hair and yanked viciously, pulling her off balance. She crashed to the ground with a grunt of pain, dropping her phone. Sliding across the floor, unnoticed, it came to rest against the leg of an occasional table.

Dropping to his knees, JJ straddled her as she lay on the floor in the hallway. He rained slaps down on her, mumbling incoherently in his anger. Willow bucked and rolled wildly underneath him, trying to unseat him. If she could just get him off her, she could run, get away. Get to her girls and safety.

She needed to keep her babies safe. She couldn't let JJ get his hands on those precious children. Renewing her efforts, she managed to unseat him and rolled away. As she gained her knees, she felt an excruciating pain in her side. His aim true, JJ landed another kick to her ribs, this one taking her back down to the floor.

Clutching her side, Willow grimaced in pain, trying to catch her breath. Grabbing her by the hair again, this time JJ slammed her head into the tiled floor. Stars exploded behind Willow's eyes, and her vision blurred, the pain almost unbearable. In the far reaches of her mind, she wondered if this was how Meri had felt the night this animal had beaten her like this.

In a frenzy of rage, he continued to rain kicks and blows on Willow. Fighting back like only a mother could, she managed to get in a few blows of her own before receiving a particularly vicious kick to the temple. Lying dazed and disorientated, there was little she could do to ward JJ off as he slammed her head into the tiles yet again.

Her sight went black, and as Willow slid into unconsciousness, her last thought was that there was no one to protect the girls, hers and Adam's.

Her cell phone, lying neglected and forgotten, continued its tinny squawk as Adam yelled down the line. There was no one to hear him.

Adam was losing his mind. As he sat listening to Willow being assaulted, impotent rage washed through him. He should have been there. All he could do was put the call on hold while he phoned the assault in. A patrol vehicle was being dispatched before he'd even hung up the call. It was police code – they always looked after their own.

It didn't do anything to make him feel better. He put his siren and lights on and floored it, thankful for the powerful vehicle. It would take him at least fifteen minutes to get to Willow and the girls – the longest minutes of his life. He couldn't remember a time when he'd felt such helpless fear, not even as a rookie policeman new on the job. Icy cold, it clamped down hard.

He needed to free up his phone, so he could be reached when necessary, but he couldn't bring himself to cut the connection. He'd heard the phone clatter to the floor at some point and realised Willow was no longer able to hear him. Still, he couldn't hang up. It felt like the only connection he had to her, no matter how tenuous.

Running red lights and stop signs, Adam raced through the quiet early morning hours like the hounds of hell themselves were chasing him. His only thought was to get to Willow's house. Nothing like a moment of panic to give a man clarity. His feelings had been muddied by the hurt he'd felt over Trisha's betrayal, but there was nothing like the knowledge of possibly losing someone special to bring one's emotions in sharp focus.

He just hoped like hell he'd get a chance to tell Willow how he felt, to apologise to her for how he made her feel when he ran away from his feelings the night before.

By the time he reached the house twelve minutes later, he was about to lose his mind with worry. He imagined every worst-case scenario he'd encountered in his long career as a policeman. He, better than most, knew how these things could end.

Coming to an abrupt stop in her driveway, Adam bolted out of his vehicle, not even bothering to lock as he ran. The front door hung askew on its hinges, wide open as it had been kicked. Uniformed personnel and security officers milled around. And just like that, Adam was hurtled into the past.

The flashing lights cutting through the night sky, the neighbours standing around outside their houses — it was all sickeningly familiar. Only this time it involved somebody he'd come to care about. Not to mention his daughter was in that house, as well as hers. They must be out of their minds with fear.

He skidded to a halt as he found an unconscious Willow lying on the floor in the hallway while an officer kneeled beside her, trying to revive her. Reaching out a hand, he lightly touched the man's shoulder, flashing his credentials when the man turned his head.

"I've got this, Officer."

"Yes, sir."

The officer moved over to make space for Adam.

"Report?"

"We arrived approximately five minutes ago, sir, after receiving the dispatch. We found the front door open, as it is, and this lady lying on the floor, unconscious. We've searched the house. There are some unmade beds in two of the rooms, indicating she wasn't the only occupant of the house. But there's no one else here now, sir."

Adam had been running his hands gently over Willow in an attempt to assess her injuries, but his head whipped around at the man's words.

"Say again, Officer?"

"Er– which part, sir?"

"About other occupants of the house."

"No one else, sir. She was the only one we found," the officer replied, pointing at Willow.

Without another word, Adam jumped to his feet and ran down the passage to the girls' room. Just as the officer had said, the beds were unmade, empty. The girls were gone. Dear God, their children were gone!

Trying desperately to distance himself so he could think, he drew in a much-needed breath he hadn't realised he'd been holding. He felt sick to his stomach. How was he supposed to think like a policeman when he was reacting like a man? This was why people like him shouldn't get involved, shouldn't have families. Because of moments like this.

Focus, damn it! Get your shit together and focus.

He hurried into Willow's bedroom, checked in the *en suite* bathroom. Of course, they weren't there. He'd known they wouldn't be there but had felt compelled to check. Returning to the hallway, Adam hung onto his composure for all he was worth. It would never do for him to fall apart now. Willow and the children needed him to be strong, to get them out of this hellish nightmare.

"Who's the senior officer on scene?"

A man, one of a group of four near the door, stepped forward.

"I am, sir. Name's Sergeant Amos Gasant."

"Sergeant, I'm Detective Adam Dawson. I'll be IO on this matter. Three girls are missing from the house. All three children are four years old. We need to get the word out to all the relevant parties immediately. They've gone missing in the last" — Adam checked his watch — "twenty minutes. The quicker we get on this, the quicker we can find those little girls."

"Yes, sir. Right away."

Sergeant Gasant went off to do as he was told. Adam went back over to Willow. Squatting down beside her again, he picked up a cold, limp hand. Rubbing to get some warmth back into it, he called to her.

"Willow. It's Adam. I need you to open your eyes for me. Come on now." He continued rubbing, calling. "Has an ambulance been dispatched yet?" he asked no one in particular.

"Yes, sir. They're on their way. ETA approximately seven minutes out."

Nodding his thanks, he turned back to Willow.

"Come on, Willow. Open your eyes for me. Please."

He continued to rub, almost mindlessly. Looking down at her beautiful face, already showing signs of the ugly bruising to come, he willed her to open her eyes.

"Willow. Please, I need you to open your eyes. The girls are gone. Willow!"

The snap in his voice seemed to do the trick. He heard a tiny moan as Willow tried to move.

"That's it, honey. Open your eyes. Come on. You can do it."

Her eyelids fluttered for long moments before she opened unfocused eyes. She went to sit up. Letting out a louder groan of pain, this time she subsided. Brushing a tender thumb beneath her split bottom lip, Adam snagged her attention.

"Hey."

Very carefully, Willow licked her badly abused lips.

"Hey yourself," she whispered. Trying again, she continued, "Adam, are the girls okay? Where are the girls? Are they okay?"

Since the second attempt was no more successful

than the first, he leaned a little closer, steeling himself to tell her that the girls had been taken.

"I— Willow—"

He couldn't get the words out. He couldn't bring himself to say the words to her, to be the one who told her their children were gone. Adam watched as tears flooded in, glazed her already unfocused gaze even more.

"No. No! Adam, please . . . Tell me he didn't take them? Please?" A single tear slipped over the bottom lid and tracked its way down her face, almost lost in the purple bruising. Another followed shortly before the rest began falling unchecked.

Clamping a hand over her ribs, Willow grimaced in pain but was unable to hold back the sobs. The heartbreak in her eyes was more than he could stand. Closing his own, he opened his mouth to answer her, then closed it again. This sweet, funny, courageous woman had already been through so much, the words he needed to say just wouldn't come.

"Please?"

The anguished whisper cut right down to the bone.

"I'm sorry, honey. All three girls are gone."

Adam felt like he was coming out of his skin. He was waiting for the ambulance to get there so they could take care of Willow so he could get to the task of finding their daughters, but it seemed to be taking an eternity.

Dealing with Willow's grief and anguish on top of his own worry was pushing him to breaking point. He needed to keep her calm though. They had no idea what injuries she might have. He smoothed a hand over her hair, brushing it out of her face.

"Shh, honey. Don't upset yourself like this. We'll find the girls. I'll find the girls. I promise."

The sound of a gurney running over the path paving caught his attention just as the sergeant he'd spoken to earlier came through the door.

"Paramedics are here, Sir."

"Thanks, Gasant. Appreciate it."

Nodding to Adam, Gasant stepped out of the doorway to allow them past. Adam too got up from where he was squatting beside Willow to allow the two paramedics to get to her. Stepping back, Adam placed a call to his partner. It was a difficult conversation, but he knew, without a doubt, that his partner had his back, and he needed him right then.

When they were ready to transport Willow to the hospital, one of the EMTs came over to where he stood.

"I understand you're the investigating officer?"

"Yeah. Dawson."

"We're ready to transport the patient. She's somewhat emotional, which is to be understood considering the trauma she's been through. Do you know if she has a family member or friend that can be notified to be with her?"

"She apparently has a brother in New Zealand, but I'm not aware of anyone local. Let me see what I can do."

"We're headed to Flatrock Private Clinic. They'll find her there."

Already dialling, Adam lifted a hand in thanks. This was the call he absolutely dreaded making. His mother was the only person he could think of asking, but it meant he'd have to tell her what the situation was. It was, by far, the hardest call he'd ever made. Even during his career when having to inform someone a loved one had died. This time it was far too personal.

CHAPTER FOURTEEN

JJ was beside himself with rage. Not only had he not been able to finish Willow off, as he had intended, but now he had an extra mouth to feed that he hadn't anticipated. None of this had gone to plan.

Instead of his daughters being happy to see him, the brats had done nothing but cry and scream since he'd snatched them earlier. It wasn't supposed to have gone like this, damn it. He was supposed to get the satisfaction of killing that bitch and getting his two daughters back. Now he was stuck with someone else's child as well.

He hadn't intended taking her but, without him knowing at first, she'd stood watching him as he started to choke the life out of Willow. The bloody child screamed the house down when the dratted woman started kicking at the floor, fighting for breath. He could neither bring himself to kill in front of the child nor kill the child. But he couldn't leave her behind either, so he'd grabbed her too. Now he had no idea what the hell he was going to do.

Thankfully, they seemed to be running out of steam. If he was lucky, they'd fall asleep soon, and he'd get some silence to think. He needed to figure out how the hell he was going to get out of this mess.

Poking his head through the door, he noticed that the children were huddled together into a corner of the couch, pressed tightly up against each other. Drawing comfort from each other probably. He withdrew his head quickly before they could spot him. At least the screaming and sobbing had finally abated, for the moment. Thank God. He needed to figure his way out of this evening's disaster – how to get rid of Willow permanently and keep the child silent without killing her. He may be many things, but a child killer wasn't one of them!

Fuck, his life sucked.

Everything hurt. That was the first thought Willow had as she opened her eyes. Adam's mom had been with her since she'd been brought up to the ward. But the guilt and grief bit so deep she had no idea what to say to the older woman – the woman had introduced herself as Violet if she remembered correctly. She'd simply clutched the woman's hand like a lifeline. Anything not to feel so desperately alone.

After the first few minutes, the medication in the drip had kicked in, and she'd drifted into blissful oblivion where she didn't have to think or feel. Now she was awake again, and there wasn't a part of her that didn't hurt. She didn't think she'd ever experienced all-consuming pain like this before.

Trying to swallow past the bruising in her throat as well as the lump that emotion had formed, Willow grimaced. It felt like she'd swallowed a boulder made of sandpaper.

Speaking wasn't easy, and the nurse had advised against it, but she needed the sound of a familiar voice. She had no idea what time it was, at home or in New Zealand, but she quickly dialled Brett's number.

"Hi, sis! How are you doing? It's a little early for you to be calling, isn't it?"

Just hearing Brett's voice, Willow couldn't hold back the sob that welled up. It hurt as it ripped out of her throat, feeling as if it was tearing her soul out with it.

"Brett... .," she eventually managed to croak.

"Wills, what's the matter? Is everything okay?

Are you okay? The girls?"

The concern in Brett's voice carried clearly down the line.

"Oh God, Brett, JJ got the girls."

Willow clamped a hand over her ribs as they protested in agony against the sawing breaths she took. She tried in vain to calm her breathing. She was too emotionally overwhelmed.

"Say what now?"

"JJ – the girls' father – he's kidnapped them." Another sob.

"Shit, Little Bit! What do you need me to do? Have you let Ma know?"

"No, and I don't intend to. I don't want her here. Don't you tell her either," was the vehement rejoinder. "I just wish you could come home. I really need you."

Because it hurt to cry, to breathe, Willow tried to hold it all in, but in that moment, she realised just how much she needed the solid strength of her brother.

"Is there anyone with you, sis? I have something I have to take care of real quick, but I'll phone you right back, okay?"

"A friend's mom is here. I don't know her, but at least I'm not alone. It's okay, Bugsy. We can talk later."

"Love you, Little Bit. I'll phone you back shortly."

"Love you too," Willow replied before cutting the connection.

Putting her phone on the bedside table, she gave in to the sobs she'd been holding back. The harsh, ugly sobs wracked her body as she lay in the hospital bed. That's how Adam found her.

Gentle, solid warmth enfolded her. Breathing Adam in, she drew in the scent that had become so familiar. It made her cry harder. He provided a safe haven for a blessed moment where she could let it all out.

Adam heard Willow talking on the phone as he walked into her ward. He was bone-weary, heartsick, and worried. Hearing how distraught she was twisted him up more inside. Wanting to comfort her but not knowing what to say, he simply toed his shoes off, carefully positioned himself beside her on the hospital bed, and wrapped her up in his arms, trying to convey what he couldn't say with action. She cried harder.

For a second, he thought he'd made it worse until he felt her burrow deeper into his embrace. She tucked her face into his neck, giving in to the heavy burden of emotion she carried. Careful not to hurt her, he held her a little closer, a little tighter. Even as he gave comfort, he drew comfort from having her in his arms.

He felt sick with worry over where his daughter

was, if she was okay. But he was more grateful than he could verbalise to have Willow alive and relatively unharmed. Yes, she was injured, scraped, and bruised, but she was alive. He was deeply thankful. All he had to do now was find their little girls.

Finally, the tears slowed, then stopped. Having cried herself out for the moment, Willow lay quietly in Adam's arms, absorbing the warmth and comfort he provided. Foggy from the medicine coming through the drip and the crying, her mind drifted, blessedly buffered from the all-pervasive fear for just a little while.

Her cell phone rang beside her on the bedside table. Adam reached over, picking it up and handing it to her. Seeing her brother's name on the display, she hastened to answer.

"Hey, Bugsy."

"Hey sis, listen up. I managed to get an emergency

visa sorted and flight out of Wellington day after tomorrow. But since I'm on the ass-end of the world, it'll take me a couple days to get there. I'll email you all the details, keep you updated as I go. Yeah?"

"Are you serious?"

"Yup. Had to call in a few favours, but I'll be headed your way in a couple of days. Wish I could be there sooner, but it's the best I can do under the circumstances."

"That's amazing. Thank you. Thank you. God, I can't wait!"

Already riding a wave of emotion way bigger than her, Willow broke down again.

"Shh, Little Bit. You'll make yourself sick, love."

"I'm just so happy you're coming home. You have no idea how much I need you."

"I'm coming. Just hang tough a little longer, sis. Okay? I'll be there before you know it. Now get some rest. See you soon. I love you."

"Love you too. See you soon."

When she'd disconnected the call, Adam took the phone from her and returned it to the table.

"Who was that?" he asked rather stiffly.

Too happy to notice the lack of warmth in his voice, Willow snuggled closer.

"My brother."

She meant to say more, but the effort was too much. Sighing tiredly, she wrapped an arm around Adam and let sleep take her. She never felt Adam's body relax under her either.

Willow was exhausted. It had been three days since JJ had snatched the girls, and she had barely slept. Adam and Gavin were working more hours than was healthy to find leads, and she hadn't heard a word from JJ. She'd been praying there'd be a ransom demand or something. Anything. She was going out of her mind with worry.

The only bright spot in her otherwise terrifying days was the fact that Brett would be arriving the next day.

Jade had arrived at the hospital the previous afternoon to take her home, and while she was grateful to be away from the hospital, she hated being home. It was a constant reminder that the girls had been kidnapped and she'd been unable to stop it. There was no describing the pain to anybody – the pain that went far deeper than the physical pain she felt.

It still hurt to move, to breathe, but she would gladly learn to live with it every day, for the rest of her life, if it meant she could have the girls back, safe and unharmed. She wished she would hear from JJ. Were the girls okay? Was he looking after them properly?

Standing at her kitchen counter waiting for a fresh pot of coffee to finish brewing, Willow had a sudden, ugly thought. *What if JJ intended selling the children?* She heard the terrible stories of women and girls being snatched every day, being trafficked for the most horrendous things. She felt physically ill at the thought. *Please God, don't let that be his plan. Please, please!*

Sliding to the floor where she stood, Willow gave in to the tears that were never far away these past few days. An inexhaustible, unending supply, it seemed. She hadn't known that the human body could produce so many. If only they helped to make her feel better. Then at least they would serve a purpose. But instead, they just added to the misery.

CHAPTER FIFTEEN

Impatiently, Willow paced in front of the living room window – impatient to see her brother. He was arriving today but had arranged a rental car he would collect at the airport since he didn't want her driving. Thanks to JJ, she'd taken quite the beating. Concussion, some nasty bruising on her ribs that made breathing hurt like hell, a few other minor injuries, assorted bruises and scrapes. The concussion had been the main concern, but thankfully, it had been given the all clear.

So she could be available to help out as, and when necessary, Jade had given their casual staff extra shifts. It allowed her to leave the shop if needed. Like today.

She was spending a bit of time with Willow while she waited for Brett to arrive. Willow had intended going to the airport to collect him, but both Brett and Adam had shot that idea down before her words were even cold. Apparently, she was meant to be resting. Like that was likely to happen. She was too worried to do more than doze fitfully.

She'd eventually given in, rather gracelessly, after arguing with them both to no avail. So here she was, pacing a groove in the floor in front of the windows. She couldn't wait to see him. It had been so long since he'd been home. Too long.

The sound of a vehicle pulling into the drive pulled her from her thoughts. Moving as quickly as she was able to, Willow headed for the front door, intending to go out to meet him. Pulling the front door open, she was met by a huge bouquet of flowers.

"Hiya, Little Bit," she heard the bouquet say.

"Brett! You're here. This is so surreal."

Poking his head around the massive bunch of flowers he held in his hand, Brett did a double take. Pretending not to notice, Willow stepped forward.

"Don't I get a hug?"

"Um . . . Are you sure it's safe for me to hug you? I don't want to damage you more."

"Just be gentle, you big lug. Now get in here and give me that hug. I haven't seen you in, like, a million years."

"And after all that time, you still haven't changed. Still giving me grief," Brett retorted laughingly.

Leaning in, he wrapped an arm around her. As Jade came up to them, he wordlessly handed her the flowers so he could wrap the other arm around his sister. Ever so gently, he pulled her in closer, holding her as if she was made of spun glass. Like she'd shatter at any moment.

Feeling overwhelmed with emotion, Willow closed her eyes and tried desperately not to cry. She had done nothing but cry for days, and she was thoroughly sick of it. As someone who seldom cried, she was annoying herself. She felt the gentle brush of Brett's fingers as he rubbed a soothing hand up and down her back and lost the battle.

"Oh, Little Bit, I'm so sorry. I don't know what to say to make it better."

Willow couldn't answer. The sobs wracked her slender frame, adding pain to misery. They stood like that for long moments, saying nothing. A silent exchange of giving and taking of comfort. Finally, the tears stopped flowing. Stepping back, Willow rubbed at her face, drying the tears, feeling like a fool for breaking down.

"How about some coffee? Or something else, if you prefer."

She'd tried to cover over her awkwardness with chatter.

"Yeah, I could do with a gigantic mug of your

coffee. Thanks.”

Mugs in hand curled up on the couch, Willow asked Brett about what he’d been up to since they’d last had a decent chat, desperate to avoid talking about what had brought him home.

“There’s plenty of time for that, Wills. Tell me what happened.”

Sighing, she started to talk. She told him everything that had happened in the last few weeks, including the threatening letters she’d received, warning her of JJ’s intentions to kidnap the children.

As the words poured from her, Willow realised just how much she’d kept bottled inside. Sharing with neither him nor Adam, all her fears and worries. Now that she’d uncorked the bottle, so to speak, everything just came flooding out. No longer able to sit still, she got up to pace. Eventually, when she’d gotten it all out, her words stumbled to an end.

Getting up from where he sat, Brett braced his

hands on Willow's arms. Placing a soft kiss on her forehead, he ran his hand up and down her arm. "Be strong, love. I have faith it'll all end well."

Willow smiled crookedly at him.

"I'm so glad you're here. Thank you for listening to me ramble. I just needed to unload a bit, to put things back in perspective, you know?"

Hearing a sound behind her, Willow stepped out of her brother's embrace to turn around. She saw Adam standing in the doorway to the living room. She'd given him a key since he was in and out, especially with the investigation and in case of emergency.

"Adam. Hi, I never heard you come in. What are you doing here?"

With a look of disdain on his face, Adam shrugged.

"I guess it's not important. Some other time, maybe. You appear to be busy."

Without another word and a last look at Willow then Brett, Adam turned on his heel and walked out.

For long seconds, all Willow could do was stand and stare at where Adam had been standing. She hadn't seen him in days, hadn't heard much from him either. Apart from random texts to check how she was doing or giving her an update on their progress, or lack thereof, he was pretty quiet.

Completely thrown, all she could do was wonder: *What the hell just happened?* He'd never looked at her like that before. Like the sight of her sickened him. Rushing to the front door, she was just in time to see Adam pull out of her driveway and speed off down the road.

Brett stepped up behind her. "What was that all about?"

"I have no idea. I've never seen Adam like that. But if I'm going to find out, I'd best go talk to him. I don't know how long I'll be – it might be a really quick trip, considering that look, or I might be gone a while. If you get hungry, there's plenty in the fridge to keep you fed."

"No worries, Little Bit. I can take care of myself. Go get your guy. Just be careful – I still don't think you should be driving, but I understand. Call me if you need anything."

Nodding her thanks, she rushed to gather her things before heading for her car. *What the hell was up with Adam?* She had never seen him look so unreachable. His eyes had been cold and flat. A person would swear she'd done something wrong. Her heart thudded in her chest as anxiety notched up. As if she really needed the added stress.

Adam couldn't remember the last time he'd been this mad. Angry, sure. But not like this. He had honestly believed Willow was different. Yet again he'd been taken in by a pretty face and a seemingly genuine heart. What was the old saying about fool me twice? It definitely seemed to be the case here. He felt like such an idiot for thinking she was different from Trisha. And because of her, his daughter was missing. He felt sick to his stomach.

Not wanting to go home to an empty house teeming with reminders that his daughter wasn't there, he drove to the station. May as well get some work done to take his mind off Willow.

After hours of fruitlessly following up bogus tips and leads about the girls' disappearance, he got in his car and drove around aimlessly. He still wasn't ready to go home to an empty house. He had no intention of going over to Willow's either. Not paying particular attention to where he went, Adam was surprised to find himself at Blouberg Beach. It had been years since he'd last been there.

Parking in the lot, he spotted a pub and restaurant across the road. He got out and locked his car before making his way over to the restaurant. Maybe a beer was what he needed. He was going out of his mind with worry about the missing children and was mad as hell at Willow. He felt helpless not being able to find their children. A feeling he loathed. Maybe having a beer or two would take his mind off the endless thoughts and fears that rolled around in his head.

He could hear people talking and laughing before he even got to the door. Apparently, even weekday evenings were popular here.

Taking a seat at the bar counter, he ordered his beer as his cell phone rang. Pulling it out of his pocket, he checked to see who it was. Seeing it was Willow, he silenced the ringing and returned his phone to his pocket. If it wasn't that he wanted to be reachable in case of news, he would just turn the damn thing off.

The bar lady sent an appreciative look his way. For a split second, he considered making a play but quickly decided against it. He wasn't in the mood for company, so he opted to ignore the flirtatious looks she was giving him, taking a pull of his beer and looking around the crowded restaurant instead.

It seemed like no time at all they were calling last round, and Adam suddenly realised he was more than a little tipsy. Reaching into his pocket, he pulled out his cell phone and called Gavin. He certainly couldn't drive in his condition.

"Hey, buddy, what's up?"

"Heya Gav, brother. Whatcha doin'?"

There was a second of silence before Gavin replied, "You okay, Adam? You sound . . . Wait, are you hammered?"

"Yeah. Yeah, hammered. That's a good way of lookin' at it."

"How many you had?"

"Huh."

"Huh, what?"

"Wait, I'm countin' quick."

Gavin laughed. Adam frowned as he contemplated how many beers he'd actually had. He hadn't been paying attention since he'd been lost in thought. He'd absentmindedly called for a beer each time the one he'd been drinking came to an end.

"Shit, bud. I don't know how many I've had. But I need you to come get me."

"Yeah, that's for sure. No point in getting your ass tossed in lock up. Where are you?"

When they'd made the arrangements, he hung up and pocketed his phone again. The bar lady moved closer.

"You could always come back to my place if you're not in the mood to head for home yet."

"Yeah, not gonna happen, honey."

She looked like he'd slapped her. Even feeling the way, he did at the moment, he still felt bad for the crappy way he'd spoken to her. She turned to leave.

"Wait up a second."

Turning, she gave him the death stare but never said a word.

"Look, I'm sorry. It's been a supremely shitty couple of weeks. Still, you didn't deserve that."

She nodded. With a last look, she turned and walked away. The mellow buzz he'd had going on from the beer evaporated. Rubbing a hand tiredly over his face, he contemplated the beer in front of him. What the hell was he going to do? Time and distance had given him a little perspective.

Surely he hadn't read Willow so wrong? If he gave her the benefit of the doubt, gave her a chance to explain, would she tell him the truth? Trisha had lied every time she opened her mouth. She'd cheated on him, then lied about it each time he'd found her out. But in the short while he and Willow had been dating, she'd never once given him a reason to believe she was like his cheating ex-wife.

Blowing out a breath, Adam acknowledged that

he might have overreacted. Which would mean he owed her an apology. Taking out his phone again, he looked at how many missed calls he had from her. Seven.

He'd have to talk to her eventually. But tonight wasn't the night for it. He'd had way too much to drink. All he wanted to do was go home and let the alcohol anesthetise him enough to get some sleep. He needed to be on his game tomorrow if he was going to continue looking for the children.

He spotted Gavin heading his way as he turned to survey the restaurant again. Standing up, he had to take a moment to steady himself. It had been a while since he'd tied one on like he had tonight, but he couldn't believe how hard it had hit him. It took him a long moment to think back over his day. Eventually, it dawned on him the last time he'd eaten was breakfast. No wonder the booze had affected him so much.

Giving his friend a lopsided grin, he started towards him.

"Ready to rock?" Gavin asked.

"Ready. Thanks, Gav. I appreciate you coming to get me."

"No problem, man. You're just lucky I didn't have a hot date tonight. Otherwise, I'd let you walk home."

Laughing, they headed for Gavin's truck.

CHAPTER SIXTEEN

Tired and disheartened, Willow started her car. She'd sat outside Adam's house for hours, waiting for him to come home. She'd phoned him repeatedly, but each time the call went to voicemail. Pulling away from his house, she headed for home.

She really didn't need this crap right now. She didn't even have a clue what the hell she'd done wrong. Working up a good mad, she thought of every curse word she'd ever heard and used it.

Not usually one for swearing, it felt good to blow off steam for a minute. She felt like they'd been living in a pressure cooker for the last few days with no release valve. Still, she was at a loss to explain what had happened earlier at her house. What was Adam so mad about?

Surely, he couldn't be angry with her for telling Brett what had been going on? That didn't make sense. Then again, nothing about this situation made any sense. If only she'd been able to talk to him about it, she was sure they'd have resolved whatever the issue was.

Running out of swearwords, Willow went back to worrying about where Adam was. Was he okay? She shuddered at the thought that he might have gotten into an accident considering the mood he'd left in. She hoped he at least was safe since she had no idea if her babies were.

Pulling into her driveway, she hit the remote to open the garage. While she waited, she looked over at the house and spotted Brett standing at the window with Jade. She sighed. She was very fond of Jade, but right now was not a good time for company. Parking her car, she sat for a while after turning the engine off, trying to gather herself.

"Everything okay, Willow?"

Not expecting anyone to come looking for her, Willow jerked upright. Turning her head, she saw Jade standing beside her door. She pulled the keys out of the ignition, gathered her things, and got out of the car.

"Yes, fine, thanks, Jade. Thanks for staying and keeping Brett company."

They headed into the house, chatting as they went. Making small talk with Brett and Jade, Willow's mind wandered. Should she try calling Adam again? Would he answer?

"Willow?"

"Hmm?" she replied rather vaguely, thoughts still centred on Adam.

"Willow! You're not even paying attention," Jade grumbled

"Sorry, Jade. I'm really tired. If you'll both excuse me, I think I'll go take a bath to soak this aching body of mine and go to bed."

Giving her a somewhat worried look, Brett nodded.

"Sure. Yeah. Sounds like a good plan. Night, Wills. Sleep tight."

"Thanks. Night guys."

"Night Willow," Jade replied.

Closing her door behind her, Willow sagged back against it, thankful that no one had asked any awkward questions she couldn't answer. She headed for the bathroom. While water filled the tub, she undressed. She let the items fall to the floor where she stood in front of the full-length mirror on the bathroom wall.

Turning this way and that, Willow cast a critical eye over the bandages and bruises that covered her body. She'd worn long pants and a loose-fitting, three-quarter sleeve top to hide the worst of it from her brother. The man was worried enough about her without having to know the full extent of the damage JJ had inflicted.

The water at the right level, Willow closed the taps. Carefully, she climbed into the bath, lowering herself gingerly into the warm water. It flowed over her abused body, causing her to hiss in momentary discomfort before she adjusted to the temperature difference.

Once the initial discomfort passed, the hot water relaxed tight muscles, eased aching bones, and soothed the many bruises. Bliss. If only she could stay in here, hiding from the world. She could pretend all was well in her life instead of having to face the reality of her current situation. She could pretend her world wasn't collapsing around her.

When the water started going cold, she climbed out of the bath, towelling off carefully. Pyjamas on, she crawled into bed, exhausted. Knowing she probably wouldn't get much sleep, she was determined to give it a try anyway. Maybe if she read a page or two, it would help her get to sleep.

After reading the same page for the ninth time, Willow gave up. Putting the book on her nightstand, she turned the light out and lay in the dark, listening to the murmur of Brett's and Jade's voices. She was surprised Jade was still there. Apparently, the two of them had hit it off better than she'd realised.

She came awake with a start. What had woken her? Her nerves rattled, she reached for her phone to check the time and saw a message notification on her screen. That must be what had woken her. Opening it, she felt ill as she read the words.

JJ: Willing to trade. You for the whiny blonde brat. I keep what's mine. You got 10 min to decide. Otherwise, I'm gonna kill her 'cos she won't shut up. And don't even think about involving your new lover boy 'cos I'll kill them all.

Blood running cold, Willow's mind raced. Would he do it? Was he really cold-hearted enough to go through with it? She didn't think so. But was she really willing to risk the child's life by calling his bluff?

Making a quick decision, she dialled Adam's number, praying he would answer this time. But, again, it rang to voicemail. Dropping her head back against the headboard, Willow knew she couldn't ignore JJ's message. He was so unpredictable. She couldn't be sure he wouldn't carry out his threat.

She messaged him back.

Willow: Where and when? Will have to wait until it's safe to leave without being seen though.

While she waited for a response, Willow slipped out of bed and dressed in warm clothing. When she heard her phone chime a message, she pounced on it.

JJ: Midnight. Parking lot of the supermarket on Lavis Drive, Bishops Lavis. Don't be late.

Quietly freaking out, Willow texted back.

Willow: I'll be there. Just please don't hurt her.

Putting her phone down, she bent to pull her sneakers on. As she finished tying the second lace, her phone chimed again.

JJ: That's all on you, bitch. You arrive on time, she lives. And you better remember to come alone. I'll kill all of them if I think you got company.

Willow checked the time. Her cell phone told her it was only a quarter to eleven. It gave her a bit of time to figure out how she was going to get out of the house undetected. Hearing footsteps coming down the passage, she quickly turned her light out, hopping back under the covers.

Pretending to be asleep, she waited as she heard a light tap on her door.

"Little Bit, you still awake in there?" She heard her brother ask through the door.

Laying quietly, she waited until she heard him

walk away. Letting out the breath she'd been holding, Willow worried at her thumbnail. How the hell had things gone so wrong for her in such a short time?

Quickly she typed out a reply to JJ.

Willow: I'll be there, alone. Like I said, just please don't hurt her.

Her thoughts turned to Adam. Should she try to reach him again? If she did, would he even bother to answer her call? She had no idea what she was going to do about him. Was he still mad at her, or had he been called in to work again? Why wasn't he taking her calls, and why the hell was he so angry? But this was his daughter, her life on the line. She couldn't *not* phone him.

The last time Willow had felt such intense panic was the year Meri had died, and she'd not only found herself without her soul sister but the mother of two tiny babies she wasn't prepared for. For someone who prized control above all else, Willow felt adrift in a sea of uncertainty and fear. Swamped, overwhelmed by it.

Checking her phone for the umpteenth time, she saw it was twenty past eleven. If she was going to make the fifteen-minute drive to Bishop Lavis in time and find the meeting place, she was going to have to leave soon. Taking a deep breath, she swung her legs over the side of the bed, sitting up. Swallowing her pride, Willow tried Adam again.

This time when it went to voicemail, she decided to leave him a message.

"Adam, it's Willow. By the time you get this message, I'll probably have met up with JJ already. You need to come get Gracie. I've agreed to trade myself for her, and JJ intends leaving her at the supermarket on Lavis Drive. I'm not sure what happened this afternoon, but I hope we get a chance to talk about it sometime. In the meantime, please come get Gracie. It's dangerous for her to be alone, and JJ won't care that she is."

Hanging up, she made her way to the door and cracked it open. Listening for any sounds from the living room, she heard nothing. Opening the door a little more, she peered around it to find the entire house in darkness. Obviously, Jade had gone home and Brett to bed.

Carefully, she made her way down the passage to the kitchen. She took a moment to rummage around in a drawer for pen and paper. Scribbling a quick note to her brother, she folded it and left it on the counter next to the kettle for Brett to find in the morning. If she couldn't get through to Adam, maybe he could. She was sure that's who her brother would call when he discovered her gone. At least, she hoped so.

She grabbed her keys off the rack by the door before letting herself into her garage. Coming to a stop just inside the door, Willow contemplated her vehicle, and she wondered how she was going to get it started without waking her brother.

Could she maybe roll it out and down the driveway, to start it in the street where it would sound like just any other car starting? Steeling herself against the pain, she decided that's what she would do.

Unlocking the car door, she climbed in. Sticking the key in the ignition, she turned everything on, moved the gear lever into neutral and let down the handbrake, while waiting for the garage door to open. Pushing off with her leg, she gave an almighty shove to get the car moving. As it started rolling down the drive, she kept an eagle eye on the kitchen door.

The vehicle ran out of momentum at the end of the driveway. Hoping it was enough not to wake Brett, she hit the close button on the garage door and started her car. Pulling the rest of the way out the drive, Willow made her way to the stop sign at the end of her road before pulling over to enter the address of the meeting spot into her phone's GPS app and catch her breath.

Having to breathe shallowly due to her aching ribs, she was out of breath from simply pushing her car from a seated position. How pathetic was that? She hated feeling this way. Well, this and so many other shitty things about her current situation.

Setting her phone to silent, she checked the time again before pulling away from the stop sign. She didn't want to be late and risk JJ making good on his threat. The panic and fear she was battling so hard to keep under control had her gripping the steering wheel with white-knuckled force. She couldn't show JJ her fear, but she was quietly losing her mind with it. If it meant saving Gracie though, she would do it again in a heartbeat.

The GPS guided her to where she needed to be, and as she approached the supermarket parking lot, Willow scanned to see if she could see JJ. The dark made it almost impossible to see anything much as many of the street lights had been vandalised and were no longer working. Bishop Lavis was rife with gangster activity and other assorted crime. It was best to stay out of the area once it got dark. He couldn't have picked a better place to commit criminal activities.

He'd instructed her to leave her car parked way in the back of the lot, well away from any light. She was to wait there until he came to her door. The thing that probably terrified her the most was leaving Gracie here, alone and defenceless, until someone found her and got her to safety. It was unsafe for a child to be left alone, but JJ didn't care. Willow prayed with everything in her that Adam got her voicemail and came looking for his daughter. It would break her heart if anything happened to the little girl because of her.

Doing as she was told, she parked right at the back

of the lot, farthest from any light. She switched the car off to wait. It was three minutes to midnight. She was sure she wouldn't have long to wait, considering how impatient the man was. JJ had always been about instant gratification.

She was wrong. By the time quarter past midnight rolled around, Willow was about coming out of her skin. He should have been there by now. Had he played her? But to what end? Here she was, sitting in the dark, and nobody knew she was there. If anything happened to her, nobody would be any the wiser for hours yet.

Adam was her only hope. She hoped he listened to her voice message.

Willow startled violently at the banging on her window. Squinting through the dark, she saw it was JJ. She took a calming breath and looked around to find Gracie. Not seeing the child anywhere, she had to swallow down the bile as Willow realised it was highly likely she'd been conned.

It had never even entered her mind that the bastard might be lying to her. She'd taken him at his word that he would release the child if she changed places with her. What a fool she'd been. Knowing him the way she did, she should have known there was a strong probability he was lying.

"Get out of the car, bitch. I'm not telling you twice," JJ barked at her.

She watched as he reached around to his back. Her heart clenched when she saw the gun he withdrew from the waistband of his jeans. With a shaky hand, she reached for the door handle.

"I'm coming out."

As she turned in her seat to get out, Willow pulled the keys out of the ignition. She locked her car on autopilot. JJ reached out and snatched the keys from her hand.

"I'll hang on to those. I wouldn't put it past you to

use them as a weapon."

The thought hadn't even crossed her mind, but now that he'd mentioned it, she mourned the loss of opportunity. With a rough hand, he patted her down. Looking for a cell phone or anything she could possibly use as a weapon. Willow silently thanked her lucky stars the weather had turned cold in the last few days. The clothing she wore was relatively bulky and concealed her cell phone from cursory detection.

Maybe she still had a chance to get out of this, with the three children. Sending a prayer heavenward, she preceded JJ as he indicated for her to do.

"The car's back there. Move it."

For emphasis, he shoved her in her upper back with his gun. Looking over her shoulder to see where he indicated, Willow didn't see the rather large stone in front of her. Standing on it, she wrenched her ankle. Crying out in pain, she stumbled but managed to stay on her feet. Showing no mercy, her jabbed her with the weapon again.

Limping, she nevertheless continued to the vehicle. She didn't intend giving him a reason to shoot her. She doubted he'd hesitate. Willow had yet to meet someone with a shorter fuse. Breaths coming short, she said a silent thank you when he finally instructed her to stop beside a well-rusted, battered-looking car.

Thrusting the keys at her, he said, "Get in and drive."

Eyes tearing in pain and frustration, Willow never noticed the teenage boy sitting a short distance away, huddled into the shadows. Unlocking the driver's door, she got in. After a moment's hesitation, while she debated the wisdom of making a run for it, she finally reached over and unlocked the passenger door.

Antagonism stamped all over his pockmarked face, a legacy of puberty, JJ climbed in.

"Don't even think about it. I won't hesitate to kill

the child if you run."

Willow held her silence. It wouldn't pay to provoke him further. She turned the key, and after a few attempts to start the car, the engine finally fired. Following JJ's directions, they pulled up outside a semi-detached, faded pink house, the peeling paint harshly highlighted by a bare bulb hanging from its electrical cord.

"Pull around the back of the house," was all JJ said as he indicated the driveway she needed to turn into.

Following it, she pulled in at the back of the rather dilapidated-looking house. Willow sat for a moment, trying to breathe through the pain in her ankle. JJ got out and aimed the weapon at her again. Taking the hint, Willow climbed out and hobbled over to where he stood.

Shoving her again, he set off towards the back door. As they reached it, she could hear the sound of a child crying hysterically. Her heart clenched, hard, as she realised the child crying was Chelsea.

"Why is she crying like that? What did you do to my baby?" Willow snarled at JJ.

Without responding, he simply backhanded her across the mouth. Not expecting the blow, she staggered back before losing her balance, landing hard as she fell. She lay there, disorientated, her face stinging. She could taste the bitter copper tang of blood in her mouth.

Gathering herself, she climbed painfully to her feet. Not giving up she repeated, "I asked you why my child is crying."

Shoving the gun hard against her cheek, he replied, "I suggest you keep your mouth shut before I blow your head off and just be done with it. You got the keys; open the door."

With shaking hands, she lifted a key to the lock. Finding it was the wrong one, she tried again. On her third attempt, Willow finally found the right key. Her nerves crawling just below the surface of her skin, she frantically worked the key in the lock until the mechanism eventually turned. Flinging the door open, she hobbled into the room as quickly as she could, looking around for her children.

Finding herself in a kitchen, she moved to the door to continue her search. In a distant part of her mind, Willow kept expecting to feel the bite of a bullet, but finding her children was her overriding priority. Throwing caution to the wind, she called out their names.

"Mommy!" Kelly screamed.

Moving into the passage, she ran towards where she thought the little voice had come from, ignoring the bite of pain. The short passage ended in a living room where she found all three children huddled together. Falling to her knees beside the couch they were on, Willow pulled all three into her arms, tears of relief tracking down her face. They were alive. Apart from a bruise or two and needing a good bath, they seemed to be unharmed.

Cradling the children to her, she offered up a prayer of thanks that she had them in her arms once more. She'd feared she would never see them again. Rocking them gently from side to side, Willow comforted the children. If only there was someone to offer *her* comfort and tell her everything would be well, but deep down she feared this wouldn't have a happy ending.

CHAPTER SEVENTEEN

Slapping an unforgiving hand on his cell phone to silence his five thirty alarm, Adam groaned. It had been a long, long time since he'd last had a hangover, and this one was a humdinger. Rolling to sit on the side of the bed, he rubbed his hands over his face. What he needed was coffee and pain pills to get his sorry-self going. Just because he'd been stupid enough to overindulge like some greenhorn teenager over a woman, didn't mean work was going to give him a break.

He picked up his cell phone, curious to see if Willow had tried to reach him the night before and saw there were several missed calls and a large number of messages. He considered ignoring it all, but the policeman in him was too ingrained. There might be something urgent. Or even something about Gracie. And to be honest, he was kind of hoping she had tried to reach him.

Dialling in to his voicemails, he decided the messages could wait for later. The first couple were hang-ups with no message, but the third one made his blood run cold. It was, indeed, Willow. But it wasn't the empty apologies he'd been expecting. Unsure whether his mind was playing tricks on him in his hungover state, Adam replayed the message.

Worry now eating at his gut too, he played the next message. And the next. By the time Adam was done listening to the handful of messages Willow had left, he was in a cold sweat. After the last one, he replayed them all. Hoping, wishing it was all just a terrible dream.

The automated voice was replaced by Willow's

fear-filled voice.

"Adam, it's Willow. By the time you get this message, I'll probably have met up with JJ already. You need to come get Gracie. I've agreed to trade myself for her, and JJ intends leaving her at the supermarket on Lavis Drive. I'm not sure what happened this afternoon, but I hope we get a chance to talk about it sometime. In the meantime, please come get Gracie. It's dangerous for her to be alone, and JJ won't care that she is."

A beep indicated the end of the message and the automated voice was back, giving him options on saving, deleting, or returning the call. Then the next message began to play.

"Adam, I really, really need you to contact me urgently. JJ's made contact about Gracie. I need your help. Please call me."

The next message began to play.

"Adam, please. I have no idea why you're mad at me, but please, please call me. JJ is impatient and won't be put off. Where are you? Please call me."

But it was the final one that made him feel ill as he listened to not just the words of the message but the tears he could hear in her voice.

"I can't wait anymore. JJ wants to trade, me for Gracie. And he won't be put off any longer. I'm going to meet him. You have to come get Gracie. She won't be safe. He said the supermarket parking lot off Lavis Drive in Bishop Lavis. I have to go. I don't trust JJ, and I have no idea how this is going to end. If anything happens to me, I trust you to keep the children safe. I have to go. Goodbye Adam."

Frantically, Adam threw clothes on, dashed into the bathroom to brush his teeth and knock back a couple of pain pills before running for the door. He needed to get hold of Gavin, but, more importantly, he needed to get on the road.

He was absolutely sick to his stomach as he realised Willow had left that message six and a half hours ago. On the off chance JJ had kept his word, what would have become of Gracie in those hours? Anything could have happened to his little girl, and it would all be his fault for behaving like a fool last night.

Backing out of his garage at high speed, he skidded to a halt to close the door and dial Gavin's number, cursing as his shaking hands made him clumsy. It took two attempts to dial right, wasting precious seconds.

"Hey, my man, you're calling early for someone who tied one on so spectacularly last night."

"He's got them all, Gav. That fucker's got all of them. We need to find them."

"Wait, what? You're not making sense. Who's got whom?"

"Jonson. He's got the kids, and now he's got Willow."

"Hold up. Jonson's got the kids *and* Willow? Are you sure? How do you know?"

"There's no time to get into it now. I'm en route to the supermarket on Lavis Drive. It's Willow's last known location. Meet me there. I'll tell you everything when you get there."

"I'm on my way. Just don't do anything stupid before I get there."

"I'll see you there."

"Adam—"

"Yeah, yeah, I hear you. Nothing stupid. Got it.

Just get there!"

Disconnecting the call, Adam threw his phone onto the passenger seat and accelerated. Time was not on his side. Thankfully, the traffic was light at that time of day. As it was just before the early morning peak hour, he managed to make good time to his destination. He knew his way around the area as it fell under his station's jurisdiction, so he knew exactly where he needed to be.

Fear, as he had never known in all his years as a police officer, was a living, writhing beast within him. Where was his daughter? Had the bastard kept his word and released Gracie, leaving her to fend for herself in an area so rife with danger? Or had he been true to his nature and lied, keeping the child and taking Willow too?

As much as he hated to think it, Adam prayed for the latter. He couldn't bear the thought of his daughter wandering around, lost and terrified, all alone. A target for anyone to snatch her. At least if she was still being held captive, he knew Willow would be with her.

Pulling into the parking lot of the supermarket, Adam scanned it to find Willow's car. Spotting it right in the back of the lot, he drove over to it and parked. He scanned the surrounds, taking in the lay of the land with the sharp gaze of a seasoned policeman, missing very little in that first sweep.

Finally, he stepped out of his vehicle, making his way over to Willow's car, careful not to touch anything. He didn't want to contaminate any evidence they might possibly find that could point straight to JJ, because this time he was taking him down. It had been a long time coming, but he was determined the man wouldn't get away with it again.

Hearing a car pull into the parking lot, Adam turned to see who it was. Finding it was Gavin, he felt a slight lessening of the sick feeling that had been churning in his stomach since he'd heard the very first message from Willow. He waited for his partner to park and join him.

When Gavin got to where he stood, his assessing gaze had Adam shifting uncomfortably. The man had a way of looking at you that made you want to confess to crimes you hadn't committed just so he'd stop staring at you like that. Eventually, he spoke.

"You hanging in there?"

Adam shook his head. He couldn't find the words to tell Gavin what he was feeling — the fear, the anxiety, the sheer helplessness of not knowing. His friend nodded.

"What do we know so far?"

"Not much. I've only just got here. But this is what I do have."

Adam took his phone out of his pocket, dialled in to his voicemail service, and put his phone on speaker so Gavin could listen to Willow's messages.

As they listened, Adam watched emotions shift across Gavin's face, a rarity as the man had perfected the art of being unreadable. It was one of his most effective tools as a detective.

The man's jaw was clenched so hard by the time they were done listening that Adam feared he might shatter teeth. His friend looked him dead in the eye, and without expression in his voice or on his face, calmly informed him, "When we find this bastard, it's going to give me immense pleasure to break him. And make no mistake, we *will* find him, and I *will* break him."

Said with such conviction, Adam believed him. Gavin was now a man on a mission, and nothing would stop him achieving his goal. But that suited him just fine because now he was done fooling around with this. He was equally determined to put an end to this cat and mouse game that had been going on for more than four years.

"I'm with you, Gav. I want this done too."

"So, what do we know so far?"

"We know she came here at Jonson's instructions. Considering he chose this particular spot, I'm guessing he would have picked it for a reason. Probably convenience, possibly proximity. Let's start there and see where we go from here."

Gavin didn't speak for a moment, and then he looked his partner and friend in the eye.

"You know you shouldn't be involved in this, right? You could compromise the integrity of this case if it ever goes to court."

"Yeah, I know, but how am I supposed to sit this one out? He's got my family, Gav. You know I can't just sit back and do nothing."

Gavin simply nodded.

"We'll figure it out. Right, so where do we start, brother?"

"I got here a couple minutes ahead of you. I

didn't even get a chance to have a look around, see if there's anything that might give us any clues. I'm going to have a look around the car."

A slight noise behind him had Adam reaching for his weapon, swinging towards it. Standing a short distance away was a young boy with his hands up.

"Sorry, mister. Don't shoot."

Adam moved his hand away from his weapon, holding it palm up. Not perceiving a threat from the boy, he started to turn back to Willow's car.

"Hey mister, are you guys the police?"

Turning back to the boy, Adam studied him before replying, "Yes, we're police officers. Do you have a problem, son?"

Ignoring his question, the boy went on. "Are you looking for the lady that belongs to that car, mister?"

That got his attention. And Gavin's too. With two sets of "cop eyes" trained on him, the youngster shrunk in on himself a little and seemed on the point of bolting. Not wanting to risk losing any possible avenue of finding Willow, Adam clamped a firm but gentle hand around his painfully thin arm. Trying to keep his voice calm and non-threatening, he asked, "Do you know anything about what happened to the lady who belongs to this car?"

At first, it didn't seem like he would answer. He simply stared at Adam and Gavin with his eyes gone big in his small face.

"We won't hurt you, son. We just really, really need to know what happened to the lady. Do you know anything?"

Slowly, the boy nodded.

"First, what's your name, buddy?"

"Tyrone, mister."

"Do you know what happened to this lady, Tyrone?"

Again, he nodded.

"Let's hear it then. What happened?"

"Before I tell you, you have to promise that he won't find out it was me who told you. He'll kill me for sure if he knows it was me. Like he almost did to my daddy."

Adam felt for the youngster. He could see how much courage it was taking to stand there and talk to them and not run as far away from the "cops" as he possibly could. The community of Bishop Lavis was a tight-lipped one for fear of reprisal should they speak to the police.

"I promise not to tell anyone who told us. Who will kill you, like he tried to kill your daddy?"

"That man, Mr JJ. He's a bad man. He does bad things to people. All the time."

The mention of Jonson's nickname had the atmosphere going wired. Adam and Gavin stepped closer to the child. He shrunk back a little farther.

"No, no. It's okay. Sorry. We didn't mean to scare you, Tyrone. Tell us what you know. We promise to keep it our secret. We won't let JJ hurt you. Okay?"

Giving the two of them a penetrating look, with eyes far older than they should be for one who appeared to be in his early teens, Tyrone seemed to be debating whether he could trust them or not. Seeming to come to the conclusion that he could, he started nodding.

"Okay."

"Do you know what JJ's full name is?"

"I only know him as Mr JJ or Mr Jonson. I don't know if he's got another name."

Pulling his notebook out of his inner jacket pocket, Adam asked, "Can you tell me what he looks like?"

The boy described the man he knew as "Mr JJ or Mr Jonson," and Adam looked over at Gavin.

"That's our man, bud."

"Yeah, it certainly sounds like it." Looking back at the boy, Gavin spoke directly to him. "Did you see the lady that belongs to the car?"

"Yes. She came here last night. And Mr JJ came and took her away. He pushed her, and she hurt herself. He was mean to her. If you're the police, you have to go get her, mister. He'll hurt her or kill her for sure if you don't." The more Tyrone spoke, the more agitated he got. "Like he did to my daddy. He came to my house, and he made my daddy go with him. And then he tried to kill my daddy. My daddy still isn't right since he shot him. I hate Mr JJ. You have to make him pay for what he did to my daddy, and the lady."

Listening to Tyrone's words, Adam's gut tightened. His fear for Willow and the girls' safety ratcheted up a few notches. He knew what Jonson was capable of. And it scared the bejesus out of him.

"Okay, okay. Just take a breath there, buddy. We'll get him. How old are you Tyrone?"

"I'm fourteen."

"Why were you out so late last night that you saw what happened with Mr JJ and the lady?"

At first, it appeared the youngster wasn't going to answer, but eventually he replied, "My ma and me had a fight, so I came to sit here so she could cool off. She gets real mad sometimes, and then it's best to just disappear for a while, you know?"

Nodding, Adam said, "Just be careful, okay. You know it's dangerous here at night, yeah?"

Tyrone nodded.

His heart in his throat, but needing to know, Adam continued, "Did you see any children with Mr JJ last night son?"

Tyrone shook his head. "No mister. It was just him and the lady."

Closing his eyes against the slice of pain at the boy's answer, he nodded.

"So, do you know where Mr JJ might have taken the lady?" Gavin asked.

Tyrone nodded.

"Probably his ma's old house."

Adam and Gavin's excitement was almost palpable. For the first time since the three girls had been kidnapped, there was a solid lead. There was hope. Who would have thought the gods would be smiling on them like this on a crappy, overcast morning? With the boy's help, taking JJ down might actually happen sooner rather than later.

"Can you show us where his ma's house is, Tyrone?" This time it was Adam who spoke to the boy.

"I know where his ma's house is, mister. But if I go with you, he'll see me, and he'll know it was me who told you, and he'll kill me."

The boy's fear was a living, breathing energy they could feel. It was clear this man needed to be stopped. Now. He'd hurt too many people. He was still hurting people. And it needed to end.

Adam bent forward at the waist so he could look Tyrone directly in the eyes.

"Tyrone, we promise you he won't hurt you. We won't let him. We'll do everything we can to make sure he doesn't know it was you who helped us. But that man has my girlfriend and my children. I need you to show me where he is before he hurts any of them. Can you do that for me?"

"He's got your babies too?"

"Yes. He's got my babies too."

"How old are you babies, mister?" Tyrone whispered, his eyes rounded in horror.

"They're only four years old, Tyrone. I need to bring them back home. Will you help me? Please?"

"Yeah, mister. I'll help you! I don't want him to hurt your babies. I'll show you where his ma's old house is."

"Thank you, Tyrone. I appreciate it," came Adam's heartfelt reply. "My car's over here. You can ride with me."

As one, Adam and Gavin turned toward their vehicles.

"I'll follow you, Adam."

Showing thumbs up, Adam unlocked his vehicle with his remote and gestured for Tyrone to hop in the back.

"If you get in the back, you can hide behind my seat as you direct me. That way no one can see who is helping me, okay?"

"Okay," was all Tyrone replied, fear clear on his face.

Before the boy could climb up into the back of his SUV, Adam put a gentle hand on his shoulder.

"Tyrone."

Tyrone looked at him.

"You have no idea how much I appreciate your help. You are very brave to help me when I know how scared you are of this man. I will do everything in my power to protect you and make sure you stay safe. But I need you to know I really appreciate you helping me."

Adam saw some of the tension drain out of the youngster's narrow shoulders. Smiling encouragingly at the boy, he again gestured for him to climb in.

"All right, son. Let's get going."

Impatience ate at him, but he sensed it was important to take a moment to reassure Tyrone. He was glad he had. But now he needed to get moving. He needed to find his family. Despite the gravity and urgency of the situation, the thought gave Adam pause. In that moment, he realised how true that statement was. His experience with his ex-wife had coloured his view on love, fidelity, and commitment, but the gravity of his present situation had opened his eyes to the fact that not all women were the same.

Willow's selfless sacrifice for a child who wasn't even her own had brought the realisation that he'd fallen in love when it was the last thing he'd been looking for. He just hoped he'd get the chance to make things right with Willow. He prayed he wasn't too late. Turning to the youngster in the back of his vehicle, Adam prayed with everything in him.

"All right, Tyrone. Tell me where I need to go."

CHAPTER EIGHTEEN

Jade rounded the counter on her way to the door to open for the day when the phone rang. Changing direction, she came around the front of it, reaching over the expanse of burnished wood to answer.

"The Reading Nook. Jade speaking. How may I assist you?"

"Jade, it's Brett."

"Hey, Brett. How goes it this morning?"

"Good, thanks. You?"

"Yeah, the same thanks. So, what's up?"

"I need a quick word with that earless sister of mine, please."

Laughing at Brett's description of Willow, she

replied, "Willow's not here though."

"She's not there? Are you sure?"

"Sure, sure. I opened up this morning. There was nobody else here."

"Huh. I wonder where she's disappeared to then. She's not here. But she didn't say anything to me about going out today. I just assumed she'd gone to the shop and not said anything because she knew I would give her shit about it. Thanks, girl. I'll chat to you later then."

"All right. Later then, dude."

Hanging up the phone, Jade headed back to the door to open for the day.

Ending the call, Brett frowned at the phone in his hand. He wondered where his sister was. Maybe she was in the bathroom and hadn't heard him knocking. Going back down the passage, he stopped outside his sister's door. Knocking again, he called out to her.

Nothing.

"Willow, are you in there?"

Still nothing. Making a decision, he turned the handle and opened her bedroom door. It was shrouded in shadows. The curtains were still closed. The bed was unmade, but there appeared to be no sound coming from the bathroom.

The quiet in the room made him uncomfortable. Where on earth was Willow?

He went over to the bathroom door that stood ajar and called out again.

"Sis, are you in there?"

But no reply came. Pushing the door farther open, Brett realised she wasn't in the bathroom either. Perplexed, he turned, heading for the kitchen. He hadn't checked to see if her car was still there. She might just be outside in the garden, getting some air. Since the girls had been snatched, Willow hadn't been sleeping well. That's probably where she was.

After finding the keys gone from their usual spot, the car gone from the garage, and no Willow in the garden or anywhere else, Brett was at a loss as to where his sister was. He'd tried her cell phone a number of times, but each time it just rang to voicemail. How the hell was he supposed to find her if she wouldn't answer her phone?

It was so unlike Willow to disappear without so much as a word to anyone. With everything going on lately though, she'd not been herself. It was understandable she was stressed and on edge. The incident with Adam the previous afternoon hadn't helped any either.

Willow had spoken so highly of the police detective every time they'd talked on the phone, but Brett had yet to see his good qualities. Yesterday, he'd behaved like a first-class dick. But she seemed so taken with Adam that Brett hoped it was the exception rather than the rule. Everyone had off days.

Glancing around the tidy kitchen again, paying closer attention this time, he noticed a folded piece of paper by the kettle he hadn't seen previously. He saw writing on it, and on closer inspection, he realised it was his name. Opening the note, Brett read.

Brett, by the time you read this, hours will have passed, but I need your help. JJ has contacted me to make an exchange for Gracie. I am going to do it. I can only pray that for once the man will keep his word. I have tried to get hold of Adam but haven't managed it yet. Please phone him as soon as you read this and tell him that I need him to come to the Bishop Lavis supermarket on Lavis Drive to look for Gracie on the off chance that JJ does keep his word this time. I love you. Wills xxx

"God dammit Willow." Brett's voice echoed in the quiet kitchen as he shouted out his anger and fear.

He threw the note onto the counter, reaching for

his phone. He redialed Jade's number.

"Reading Nook. Jade speaking. How may I assist you?"

"Jade, it's Brett again. Do you perhaps have Adam's cell number? I need to reach him urgently."

"I think Willow has it on her desk somewhere. I'll have a quick look. Is everything okay?"

"No, but I haven't got time to explain now. I need to get hold of Adam."

"No problem. Give me a sec."

He heard things being moved around and then she was back.

"Found it."

Jade rattled off the numbers. When he had them down, he thanked her, promising to call back as soon as he'd contacted Adam. Hanging up and dialling Adam's number this time, he stared blankly at the note lying on the counter while it rang.

"Dawson," was all Adam said as he answered.

"Is that Adam?"

"Yes, that's me."

"It's Brett, Willow's brother— "

"Sorry to interrupt you, Brett, but I'm in the middle of something right now. Is this something that can wait?

"No, it's urgent. This is about Willow. She's missing. I need your help. She left a note and told me to phone you."

"Yes, I know. She left a number of voicemails for me that I got this morning. That's what I'm doing now. I'm looking for her."

"Right. Okay then. I'll leave you to get on with it. Just keep me in the loop, please. I'm sick with worry for her. That JJ is a nasty piece of work."

"Yeah, he is. I'll be in touch."

The phone went dead in Brett's ear. With nothing else to be done for the moment, he decided to drive to The Reading Nook and break the news to Jade in person. They could do their worrying together. Much as he'd rather be out there helping to look for his sister, he would just be in the way, and he didn't want anything to go wrong because of him.

Hanging up, Adam threw his phone back onto the passenger seat beside him. He understood Brett's worry only too well. But he didn't have time to spare, putting the man's mind at ease. He had to find his woman and their children. That was his only priority right now.

He felt a gentle tap on his shoulder before he heard a soft, "Mister, that's the house over there."

"Which one, son?"

"The pink one there."

"Do you know if he's in there alone with the lady and the children, or if he has someone else with him?"

"I don't know, mister. I didn't see inside. I just

know he goes there when he's in the area."

Adam nodded but said nothing more. Pulling over to the curb, he cut the engine.

"Stay here, out of sight. I'm going to talk to my partner. I'll be right back."

He got out of the car, heading to where Gavin had parked behind him. Gavin was already lowering the window as Adam reached him. Bending over, Adam rested his arms on the doorframe.

"Tyrone says Jonson's in the pink one. How are we going to handle this?"

Gavin looked out the windshield, taking in the faded pink house in the dull grey of the early morning. Assessing.

"Does he know how many people are inside?"

"He doesn't know if he's in there alone with Willow and the girls, or if he's got help."

They planned logistics for a couple minutes before Adam returned to his vehicle. He climbed back in to talk to the boy but didn't turn toward him in case anyone was watching.

"Is there somewhere I can drop you off, Tyrone? I want you safe and away from here when we go in. I promised I would keep you out of it, and I intend to keep my promise."

"You can drop me off by my granny, mister. Me and my daddy have to live with her now that he's disabled because of Mr JJ."

"Around here?"

"Yes. It's close."

"All right, show me the way then, and let's get you home."

Adam followed the directions Tyrone gave him, dropping the child off at his grandmother's before heading back to the house the youngster had pointed out as JJ's hideout.

Arriving back, he parked beside the curb again and made his way over to Gavin's car, this time climbing into the vehicle. He and Gavin spent long minutes planning out how they were going to proceed, then called in for backup. Being personally involved, Adam would have to stand down from the raid of the house, but he certainly wasn't going to be side-lined from the action entirely. He would be on hand when his loved ones were rescued.

Impatience rode him hard. He was so close to those who meant the world to him without being able to do anything about it. Everything inside him screamed for him to take action, but if they wanted a watertight case against this bastard, he was going to have to sit on his hands and let his partner and colleagues take Jonson down.

Nerves tight as a drum, not able to sit still for a second longer, Adam spotted two police vehicles moving down the road toward them and stopping out of sight of the house. The driver of the front vehicle flashed his lights at them, acknowledging he'd seen them. He and Gavin got out of the car and casually walked up the road, toward the other vehicles.

The other police officers had exited their vehicles by the time they'd reached them. They gathered around for a quick debriefing before they did a recon of the house. Adam shared the limited information he had with his colleagues that his girlfriend and children were in the house, and they were to proceed with extreme caution. From all he and Gavin had learned about Jonson over the past few years, they needed to go in prepared for anything, being aware that he was dangerous and most likely armed. He wouldn't go down without a fight.

Acknowledging the briefing, the men moved to start the operation, taking Gavin with them. It took all his self-control and willpower to stop himself from joining the team of men as they crossed the road, heading for the house. They spread out, scouting the layout of the property. The most worrisome aspect was that the windows were either boarded up on the outside or where the boards had been ripped down, and the window showed, it had newspaper and cardboard covering the windows from the inside.

They were going into this blind as they couldn't see into the house, unable to get a visual on how many people were inside, where exactly they were, or if they were armed. This kind of situation always made them uneasy as it meant so many more things could go wrong during a raid.

Adam watched as a couple of the men came around the front of the house to the front door. He couldn't see the others, but knowing how these things worked, he suspected they were headed for the back door – the only other door in the structure. They would communicate via radio and coordinate the breaking down of the doors to preserve the element of surprise.

Watching as one of the men swung his battering

ram back, he felt the bile crawl up his throat. Not since his rookie days had he been this scared of the outcome of a raid. Jonson was unpredictable, and that made him all the more dangerous.

The slamming of the battering ram against the old wood of the front door tightened his nerves. Gavin was nowhere to be seen, so he assumed his partner was round the back with the other two-man team.

As the door gave under the pounding from the policeman, screams split the quiet of the early morning. Adam found himself two thirds of the way to the house when he felt a hand grab his arm. Reflexively, he swung a fist at his capturer.

"Hey, man, easy there," he heard Gavin say. "It's me."

Dropping his arm, he looked at his partner.

"You don't want to be going in there, bud. You know you can't. Hang tight. I'm going in, but I'll be back as soon as I can."

In helpless frustration, Adam watched his partner head into the house, weapon drawn. He wasn't sure which was more nerve-wracking, hearing the screams or enduring the silence that had now descended.

Suddenly, a volley of shots rang out, causing his body to jerk involuntarily. And with that, he was done waiting. He'd returned to the spot on the pavement near the vehicles where he'd been waiting initially, but now he sprinted for the house. Screw the consequences. His family was in that house. He had no intention of standing there going out of his mind. If he had to, he'd put a bullet in the bastard himself if it meant preventing him from getting off on a technicality.

Entering the house at a run, Adam skidded to a halt as he took in the scene. JJ had Willow in a choke hold around the neck, his weapon aimed at the policemen in his house. Verbal abuse and threats of violence spewed from his lips, along with spittle as he screamed at them in anger. It was when he heard the man threaten to blow Willow's head off before he'd surrender, that had Adam reaching for his own weapon.

And then it seemed as if everything happened in silent, slow motion. He watched in horror as JJ started lifting the weapon towards her head, and he realised he wouldn't get his weapon clear of its holster in time. A hole, made by a small calibre weapon, appeared in the man's forehead, along with a look of surprise on his face. His grip loosened and he began to fall to the floor. Then all hell broke loose.

The screaming started up again; men running, JJ lying on the floor, and Willow unmoving, as if she'd been turned to stone, abject terror etched on her face. As if she feared she might shatter at any moment, she slowly turned to look at the man lying on the floor at her feet. Seeing the blood now flowing from the gunshot wound in his head, it seemed to galvanise her.

She swung around, tracking the screaming, and Adam saw the moment her eyes found their target. He followed her gaze and saw the children, safe in the embrace of one of his colleagues. Safe, but terrified. As one, they moved towards the children, him reaching them a beat after Willow.

Not wanting to scare any of them more than they already were, he spoke softly.

"Willow . . ."

She turned her head. Her eyes, glazed over with shock, connected with his. It took a moment before she realised who he was. The moment the shock cleared, and her brain processed what she was seeing, he saw indecision take over – did she go to the children or him first? It took no time at all for her to make the decision, and she turned back to the three frightened pre-schoolers struggling in the arms of an unknown man in a police uniform.

Without hesitation, she sank painfully to her knees and opened her arms to receive the children from the policeman. They threw themselves into her arms, clinging to her desperately, sobs wracking their tiny bodies. Tears tracked down her face as Adam watched her pull all three into a tight embrace as if she was terrified that if she let go, their rescue would prove to be nothing more than a much longed-for dream.

Not noticing the tears that ran down his own face, Adam went to a knee beside Willow and the children, encircling all four of them in his embrace, sending prayers of thanks heavenward he was able to. There'd been sick moments in the quiet of night that he believed he wouldn't be able to find them.

He felt wetness in his neck as Willow nestled her face there. They huddled like that for a long while before she gathered her composure enough to draw back slightly from the girls in her arms. They too were starting to calm. Touching a gentle hand to Gracie's face, she whispered in the child's ear.

He was sure he experienced a taste of heaven the moment the child turned her head and her eyes connected with his, noticing him for the first time. She pulled out of Willow's embrace and threw herself at her father. He caught her and gathered her up close to his chest, holding her tight against his heart.

Movement ebbed and flowed around him as Gavin, and the other police officers went about the business of securing the scene, calling it in, alerting the crime scene investigation unit they were required. He ignored all of it as he basked in the pure joy of the moment.

Eventually, Gavin came over to the couch where they'd finally settled out of the way.

"Paramedics are here."

He pointed to where a man and woman stood

with their medical paraphernalia. Adam nodded, quietly thanking his partner before turning back to Willow.

"The paramedics are here to check you and the girls out."

It was her turn to nod. Adam indicated for the paramedics to come closer. They checked the girls first before turning their attention to Willow. Adam warned them that she had pre-existing injuries from the beating she'd received the night JJ had kidnapped the girls before she admitted that she'd hurt her ankle that night in the parking lot when she'd stumbled in the dark.

Other than having to strap her ankle after declaring it sprained, the paramedics recommended that the four of them see a doctor to be treated for the shock; otherwise, they were okay. Adam and Willow thanked them as they packed their gear.

"I'm just going to chat to Gavin quickly. I'll be

right back."

Willow nodded, but Gracie reacted badly.

"No, Daddy, please don't go," she cried.

Taking her into his arms again, he gave a hug.

"I'll be back in a minute, baby. I just need to talk to Uncle Gavin, and then, I'll be able to take you home. Okay? I promise."

Clearly unhappy about it, the child agreed reluctantly, returning to Willow's side as he stood up. He walked over to his friend, indicating for him to step slightly away from the general hubbub in the room.

"I know you need statements, bud, but I really need to get all my girls to the doctor and then home. Can you come over later or maybe in the morning for the statements?"

"Yeah, sure. Of course, my man. No worries. We can do that. I'll get this mess cleaned up and see you guys tomorrow."

"Thanks, Gav. I appreciate it."

Pulling Adam into a man hug, Gavin showed his support wordlessly. Adam went over to collect Willow and the girls. Lifting a hand in farewell, he escorted them from the scene of their emotional hell.

CHAPTER NINETEEN

After the doctor's visit, Adam had insisted on, Willow was grateful to finally be back in her own home. Brett and Jade had been there, waiting for them. One look at her beloved brother and all the emotion that had been roiling beneath the surface calm had overwhelmed her.

Without a word, Adam held his arms open to her. She didn't hesitate. She clung to him like an anchor in a storm as all that she was feeling raged through her, seeking release. He smoothed a soothing hand over her hair and gently rocked her, much as he had when she was little, offering wordless love and support, giving her silent permission to give vent to all the pent-up fear, anger, and relief. When all her tears were spent, she stood within the circle of his arms, simply absorbing the warmth.

Eventually, she gathered herself and turned toward the others in the room. Jade stepped forward and gave her a hug so tight she thought her ribs might give out. Noticing the grimace of pain, Adam gently reminded the younger woman of Willow's injuries.

"Oh God, Willow. I'm so sorry. I'm just so happy to see you. You scared the hell out of us!"

"It's okay. I get it. Believe me, I'm as happy to see you." Turning toward Adam, she gave him a nervous smile. "I never got a chance to introduce you to my brother yesterday." Gesturing to Brett, she continued, "Adam, my brother Brett. Bugsy, this is Adam."

A pained look crossed Adam's face, and Willow wondered at it. He stepped forward, offering his hand to her brother for a handshake.

"Brett, a pleasure to meet you."

Returning the gesture, he replied, "Yeah, nice to meet you."

The clipped tone of Brett's reply had Willow looking from one man to the other, not knowing why the moment was awkward. She was at a loss as to how to remedy the situation, but for now, she was just too tired to figure it out. It had been a very long forty-eight hours, and all she wanted was some pain medication and sleep. The children had fallen asleep in the car on the way home from the doctor.

"Adam, we need to get the girls in and settled. Then I'm going to go get some sleep myself. I'm exhausted."

"Yes, of course. Let's do that."

"It's okay, Little Bit. You get their beds sorted. I'll give Adam a hand bringing the girls in."

Giving her brother a grateful smile, Willow headed for her daughters' bedroom.

"I'll help you, Willow," Jade said.

By the time they'd turned the bedding down and made a makeshift bed for Gracie, Brett and Adam returned with all three sleeping girls. Brett and Jade left them to settle the girls, waiting for them in the living room. A few minutes later, Willow and Adam re-joined them.

"Jade and I've been talking, and it's been decided I'm going to spend a couple of nights at her place to give you guys some privacy," Brett said.

"But Brett…," Willow began.

"No, Little Bit. You've been through a hell of an ordeal over the last couple of weeks. You and Adam need time to sort things out too. I'll just be in the way here. By staying at Jade's, I'm still close by, but you have your space to deal with things."

Sighing in defeat, knowing she wouldn't change his mind, Willow nodded.

"Fine. But you better not be scarce. I don't know when I'll get to see you again."

"I promise," Brett laughed. "Now go get some sleep. You're about ready to fall over."

"I won't argue there."

Brett and Jade said their goodbyes and departed, leaving Willow and Adam alone for the first time in days.

"Head for bed, honey. I'll make sure the house is locked up, then I'll join you."

"Okay," Willow agreed readily.

Bone-deep weariness weighed on her. She'd been running on nothing more than fumes for hours now. But she was afraid to sleep. Afraid of what waited for her in her dreams.

Sensing his presence, Willow turned to find Adam standing watching her with an unreadable expression on his face. Holding her peace, she stood quietly, letting him look his fill, waiting for him to speak. He clearly had something on his mind. She knew he'd share when he was ready. Adam stepped forward, not saying a word. Simply looking deeply into her eyes.

Staring into her eyes, emotion swelled in his chest. She evoked a feeling of such tenderness, the likes of which he'd never experienced before. He'd been convinced she was lost to him. Now that he had her back, he couldn't express how deeply grateful he was to have her safely home again.

There were so many things he wanted to say to her, needed to say to her. Things he should have had the courage to say before instead of behaving like a jackass and almost screwing things up forever. Almost losing her forever.

He'd not given her an opportunity to explain what he'd seen the night she'd gone to JJ in the hopes of saving Gracie, yet she'd been willing to give up her life to save his daughter. Even when she believed he'd turned his back on her. He couldn't bear thinking that he could have lost her, and his last words to her were spoken in anger. There was so much he wanted to say to her, but he couldn't find the words. He'd never been a man able to find words to express himself easily.

He'd just have to show her what he seemed unable to say.

Running a gentle finger down her cheek, he felt his heart clench. God, she was so damn beautiful. That beauty shone through despite all the bruises and scrapes – the outer and, most especially, the inner beauty.

His heart ached for her, knowing how she'd earned every bruise and scrape. Saving not only her own children but his little girl too. He wanted to take all that pain and suffering away. To heal her, make her whole again. Show her how much he loved her.

Overwhelmed by emotion he wasn't used to, the best he could manage was, "Honey, I need you."

Without hesitation, Willow stepped into his

embrace. True to her nature, she gave selflessly to him even as he knew she had needs of her own. But that was okay because he intended to give back to her, a hundredfold. To give of himself, just as she gave so freely of her own beautiful self. To show her how sorry he was for behaving so badly when she'd done nothing to deserve it.

He would spend the rest of his life showing her if she would have him. He'd almost allowed the actions of one selfish woman to ruin the best thing that had ever happened, not only to him but his daughter too.

Letting go of Willow, Adam took a step back, reaching for her bulky sweater. Taking hold of the hem, he carefully removed it. Dropping it to the floor, he reached for the thinner top she had on beneath it, repeating the process. Finally, only her long-sleeved top remained. One-by-one, he slipped the buttons free of their holes, revealing the pale, creamy skin beneath.

When the last button was undone, the material lay separated, revealing a sliver of skin exposed. Taking a deep, calming breath to stop himself from ripping the rest of her clothes off and throwing her down like some prehistoric caveman, Adam lowered the top down her arms and back.

Adding it to the growing pile on the floor, he took a moment to savour the sight before him. Looking at her through a filter of love, he didn't see the marks that marred her perfect skin. All he saw was the woman who had captured his heart, who had come to mean everything to him. He helped her get ready for bed before settling in behind her, careful not to jostle her. It didn't take long before her breathing evened out in sleep. Knowing sleep wouldn't come easily, he held her a little tighter and tried to calm his thoughts. He didn't want to dwell on the last few days.

Jolting awake, Adam realised Willow was no

longer in the bed with him. He reached out to switch the light on, scanning the room. He spotted her sitting on the bench seat of her big bay window. He got up and padded soundlessly over to where she sat.

Leaning down, he placed his lips over hers. A kiss as gentle as butterfly wings. But it soon sparked something far less gentle. As passion took hold of them both, the kiss deepened until they had to pull apart to draw breath. They'd gone slow after her ordeal but now, done with going slow, they tore at each other's clothing, suddenly desperate.

Adam picked Willow up, cradling her to his chest as if she were the most fragile treasure, carrying her over to the bed. He laid her down gently before lying down beside her. Without warning, Willow pushed him, taking him to his back in surprise. Straddling him, she looked down at him.

"I never thought I'd have another chance to be with you like this again. To see you again. To tell you

I'm sorry for whatever it is you think I did when you walked out on Brett and me."

"Shh, baby. Don't. You have nothing to apologise for." His eyes darkened with emotion as he swallowed, his voice continuing urgently, "That was all on me. I allowed Trisha's selfishness to colour my view of all women, so instead of trusting you and giving you the benefit of the doubt, I jumped to the wrong conclusion. I behaved like a jealous child instead of a mature adult. That's all on me. You have nothing to be sorry for."

Tears welled in the sapphire depths of Willow's eyes.

"Adam, I . . ."

Placing a finger over her lips, Adam silenced whatever she was going to say next.

"No, honey. There's no excusing what I did."

"Oh, Adam …," Willow tried again.

And again, Adam silenced her.

"I was too blind to see it until it was almost too late. Even if I had, I'm not sure I would have had the courage to tell you first. Trisha taught me a harsh, if skewed, lesson. I used her as a yardstick in my relationships after her. Now I realise I did those poor women wrong. I don't want to do that with you anymore. You mean so much more to me. And I need you to know."

The tears now tracked down the smooth marble of Willow's cheeks. Lowering her lips to his naked chest, she placed tiny kisses there. She worked her way down over the smooth skin of his abdomen, stopping a moment when she encountered a bullet scar, before moving ever onwards.

Realising her intention, knowing he'd never last if she reached her destination because he needed her so damn bad, Adam reversed their roles again. He kissed her, pouring everything he felt, but couldn't adequately express in words, into the moment.

Willow smoothed her hands down his back as he kissed her, giving as much as she received. With each gentle stroke of his skin, Adam hardened more. He'd been trying to take things slow, but her touch did things to him.

Kissing his way down, he worked over to the firm globe of her right breast. Sucking the tightly furled nipple into the warm, wet cavern of his mouth, he revelled in Willow's swiftly indrawn breath. He nipped at the little bud, then laved it with his tongue to soothe it as he felt her hands in his hair. He felt her tug as if asking for more.

He kissed his way over to the other breast, giving it the same treatment before running his tongue down the centre of her body, making his way down to the very core of her femininity. Detouring at the last minute, he placed yet more kisses on the inside of her thighs. He made his way down one before working his way back up the other to his original destination.

Using his thumbs, he parted her swollen lips, groaning out loud when he noted how wet and ready she was for him. Blowing a gentle breath over the wetness, Adam felt Willow shiver. He ran the tip of his finger over her clit before easing it into her tight heat. She moaned, low and deep.

When he leaned in, touching his tongue to her clit, she tightened around his finger. He loved how responsive she was.

"Adam, please ...," he heard her whisper.

He responded by drawing the swollen button into his mouth. Alternately sucking and licking at her like she was his favourite ice cream, Adam built the tension, driving her higher and higher, pushing her towards the precipice. Adding another finger, he curved them, massaging the sweet spot he knew was guaranteed to push her over the edge.

Willow's fingers tightened almost painfully in his hair, then he felt her go over the edge into blessed freefall, crying out her pleasure. Gentling his movements, Adam slowly brought her back down. Giving her time to catch her breath, he slid his body over hers. As he supported his weight on his arms, she reached out to touch a hand to his whisker-roughened cheek.

"Make love to me. Please. I need to feel you inside of me."

"Give me a second."

Cursing himself for not thinking ahead, Adam hopped off the bed in search of his pants. Finding them in the tangle of clothing on the floor, he pulled his wallet out of the pocket. He yanked the condom out, ripping at the foil, desperate to open it. Willow watched avidly as he sheathed himself.

Climbing back onto the bed, he settled himself between her thighs and rested the head of his erection at the opening of her channel. Holding his gaze, communicating his love for her with his eyes, he pushed into her. Ever so slowly. Willow's eyes closed.

"No baby. Open your eyes. I want to see you. I want to watch you come undone for me again."

Opening her eyes again, she looked back up at him. He could see the pleasure and the love reflected there. And as they moved together in a rhythm as old as time, he felt it in her touch, heard it in her moans and sighs, saw it as he watched her unravel beneath him.

Adam felt his body tighten, the pleasure building. He felt the warning tingle in his spine as he drew ever closer to his release. Slowing his thrusting he brushed his thumb over Willow's clit, wanting to push her over first.

He was rewarded for his efforts when he felt Willow go slick and tight around him. Keeping up the onslaught of pleasure, he saw the moment her eyes glazed over and she came for him. She was glorious in the throes of orgasm. As her unfocused gaze clung to his, he followed her into bliss.

CHAPTER TWENTY

Willow stretched and felt all her muscles protest. She could definitely feel they'd been put through their paces last night. Just the thought brought a smile to her lips. And to think, she'd been worried about what dreams waited for her in sleep.

Feeling a gentle touch of lips on hers, she heard a soft, "There she is. Open those gorgeous eyes, honey. Let me see you."

Prying her eyes open, she saw Adam leaning over her with that seductive smile she'd come to love so much.

"Good morning, gorgeous. Sleep well?" Adam said softly against her lips.

Not feeling completely awake yet, Willow only nodded, returning his smile.

Scooping her up gently, he carried Willow into the bathroom.

"Come on then. Your shower's ready."

He undressed her and led her into the stall where the water cascaded in a warm waterfall, soothing her aching muscles. Guiding her under the spray to get her hair wet, he squirted some shampoo into his palm. With slow, measured strokes, Adam massaged the shampoo into her hair, and Willow couldn't hold back a moan of sheer pleasure.

"Like that, do you?"

"Mmm," Willow mumbled.

Laughing, Adam reached out for the body wash as he continued his task of washing her. Willow groaned again as his warm, rough-skinned hands moved over her. He had such magic hands. They were confident in their touch but so gentle, just like the man himself.

As big as Adam was, she didn't think she'd met a gentler man than him, and his confidence was a major turn on for her. After JJ's harsh treatment, it meant even more to her having a man treat her so gently. Especially since she still hurt all over from the abuse, she'd received at JJ's hands.

"Turn around, honey."

The husky note in Adam's voice brought her out of her reverie. Complying, she turned with a sigh of contentment.

"If you keep that up, Adam, I'm going to melt into a puddle on the shower floor."

"Lean back against me. I've got you," he said, wrapping his arms around her.

Leaning her head back against his shoulder, she couldn't hold back another sigh. Turning in his arms, Willow looked up into the face that would make an angel weep.

"Touch me."

Adam leaned down to lay his lips softly against hers and kissed her. Slowly, he ran his hands down her back, rubbing and massaging as he went.

"I doubt we'll have long before the girls are awake."

"Then move. More action and less talking," Willow replied on a laugh.

Placing a hand over her heart, Adam smiled back. She stilled, and laying a hand on his forearm, she halted his progress.

"Did you hear that?"

The quiver in her voice was unmistakable. Her flight or fight sense was clearly still on high alert.

"Hear what, honey?"

"That noise. I'm sure I heard something from the front of the house."

Reaching behind her, Adam turned the taps off. Stepping out of the shower, he grabbed a towel and handed another to her. Drying quickly, he left the bathroom while Willow was still navigating all the bruises and injuries to dry herself.

He moved so quietly she never heard him, wherever he'd disappeared to.

She hadn't even managed to get herself out of the shower when the girls came dashing into the bathroom, eyes wide with fear. It hurt her to see the children so afraid. But to be honest, she too feared the unknown noise.

"Mommy, we're scared," Kelly's little voice cracked.

"It's okay, baby. Mommy's right here. Just give me a minute to get dry and dressed, all right?"

The children huddled together inside the bathroom and nodded almost as one. They had no intention of budging until she was out of the shower.

By the time she'd dried off and managed to get herself dressed, she was out of breath. That's where Adam found her a few minutes later; sitting on the closed toilet, trying to catch her breath. The children clinging to some part of her.

"Brett and Jade are here. It was him you heard, banging on the door. Clearly, we were too preoccupied to hear him the first few times." Adam winked. Holding out a hand, he waited for her to take it before helping her up from where she sat.

To lighten the atmosphere, he smiled at all of them before saying, "Come on then. Let's go say hi."

Without another word, all three children preceded them out of the room. Although they were a little quieter than normal, for the most part, they seemed to be coping all right after their ordeal. Willow made a mental note to keep an eye on them, just in case.

She and Adam followed them down the passage to where they stood staring wide-eyed at Brett. Seeming suddenly unsure, they stood huddled together. Willow's heart ached as she realised that it was a direct result of what they'd been through in the past few days. Laying a tender hand on the closest child's shoulder, she urged them forward with her.

"It's okay, my sweethearts. Nobody will hurt you. Come say hello to Uncle Brett." She smiled encouragingly at the girls.

Walking over to Brett, she went up on tiptoe to give her brother a quick kiss hello. Seeing that she was so comfortable with him, the children offered shy hellos. They settled down in the living room, chatting, catching up, absorbing the gift of everyone being safely home.

When Willow noticeably started flagging, Brett spoke directly to the three little girls playing quietly at her feet.

"Who's up for ice cream and some toy shopping?"

The question was met with silence. The children turned to Willow and Adam as if seeking reassurance. Their ordeal made them more reserved than they would normally have been.

"I've got this," Adam whispered in Willow's ear.

Going down on a knee, Adam got down to their level. Pulling them in for a hug, he quietly gave them the reassurance they sought.

By the time he was finished talking to them, three voices rang out as one in excitement. No one, it seemed, was going to turn down the opportunity for either ice cream or toy shopping. With a flurry of activity, the girls were readied, goodbyes were said, and they were off. Adam dispatched Willow to her room for a nap while he saw everyone else out the door. With a blissful sigh, Willow sank down on the bed and succumbed to sleep quickly.

After checking in with Gavin, Adam had checked in on Willow to find her sleeping rather restlessly. He, himself, was feeling rather restless, unable to settle in any one spot for long. Eventually, he found himself back in Willow's bedroom. Sitting on the bench seat of the big bay window, he watched her sleep.

He'd spent most of the night awake, doing exactly the same thing. He was swamped by emotions he was unaccustomed to feeling, and it had shaken him. Much as he'd longed for the anesthetising comfort of sleep, it evaded him until the early morning hours. Finally, he'd drifted into welcome slumber when he realised fighting his feelings was futile.

Willow's kidnapping had brought into stark focus how important she'd become to him. He'd understood that life without her in it wasn't to be contemplated. He loved her, and he needed to tell her. His gaze shifted from the view outside the window back to Willow. She was waking up. Making his decision, he walked over to the bed.

Sitting on the edge of the mattress, he waited for her to open her eyes. He was the first thing she saw when she did. Leaning over, he placed a whisper-soft kiss on the shoulder closest to him, exposed by her tank top.

"Hey," her voice croaked out.

"Hey yourself, gorgeous."

Willow ran the tip of her tongue over her dry lips before smiling sleepily at him. His avid gaze followed its progress. Everything in him tightened.

"What's the time? How long have I been sleeping?"

"It's a little after three. You've only been out for about an hour. Brett called while you were sleeping. They're apparently having too much fun together to want to come home any time soon, so not to expect them back before dinner."

Giving a luxurious stretch before grimacing when every muscle and body part protested, Willow nodded but gave no reply.

"Willow, I need to tell you something. Please forgive me if I bungle it, I'm not much of a man for words. But hear me out, okay?"

"Is everything all right, Adam?" Willow's brow creased in concern.

"Yeah, all good. I just have something I need to tell you."

"Shoot." She pulled a face. "Sorry. Poor choice of words. Go ahead."

Adam laughed and shook his head. Cupping her cheek in a large hand, he got lost in the intense blue of her eyes. The eyes he loved so much.

"I thought I'd found what my dad and mom had when I met Trisha. She swore she loved me, I was her whole world, we would be together forever. She lied. When I caught her cheating, she killed every dream I'd had of having a marriage like my parents. Something in me broke that day. I never thought I'd be able to fix it. To be honest, I'm not sure I wanted to."

Placing her smaller hand over his, Willow nodded for Adam to continue.

"The first time I laid eyes on you, despite your grief, you were the most beautiful woman I had ever seen. I wanted you from that very first time with an intensity I'd never felt before. Then I got to know you as a person. That's when I realised how wrong I'd been. The promise of Trisha held no substance. She was incapable of loving anyone other than herself. You made me see not all women were like her."

"I'm sorry she hurt you so badly, Adam. Sure, there are women like her in the world, but you're right, we're not all like her. There are more who aren't like her than there are."

"You made me see that. When you went to Jonson, knowing that he was probably lying to you, to save the life of my daughter. And in a million other ways, you showed me you were nothing like her."

Adam had to take a moment as emotions welled up in him. Willow squeezed his hand gently, offering silent strength.

"With you, I've found love at last. A love that's real. One I *know* will last. The love I see between my parents. I love you, Willow. More than I ever thought possible for one person to love another. You are my everything, and I would be lost without you."

"Adam, I . . . Wow!" Willow took a moment. "The look on your face when you walked out that day, I thought you despised me. Then when I was at JJ's mercy, I thought I would never get to see you again. The one regret I had all the while was that I never told you I loved you. How much you mean to me. I love you, Adam."

Mindful of all the bumps and bruises, Adam took Willow into his arms. What started out as an easy kiss quickly turned heated. Rolling to his back, he took Willow with him so she wouldn't have to bear his weight. As she kneeled above him, he ran feather light hands up and down her back.

Eventually breaking the kiss to come up for air,

Adam laughed with the sheer joy of having her in his arms.

"Much as I'd like to get into it with you right now, honey, I think we'll be getting company shortly."

"You're right. Besides, we've got the rest of our lives to look forward to." Willow smiled in return.

"Yes, we do. And I can't wait. In the meantime, while we wait for the munchkins to get home, let's go see what we can scrounge up to eat. I'm starving. We've not had breakfast yet, and you wore me out last night, woman."

Laughing at him as he walked toward the door, Willow threw a pillow at him. Grinning that cocky grin, he knew she secretly loved so much, Adam held out a hand to her. She got up, taking his hand as she reached him. Walking together down the passage to the kitchen, Adam savoured this moment, the first of what he knew would be many, with his Willow beside him.

ACKNOWLEDGEMENTS

This book is the culmination of a dream and hard work, but I could not have told Adam and Willow's story without love and support. I will be forever in their debt - my thanks to:

To my mom, my husband and my son for never wavering in their belief that I could do it. Even when I doubted myself. Grant, thank you for cracking that whip, my boy. It is more appreciated than you know. Thank you all for holding me accountable to my dreams, goals and deadlines. I love you.

To Raymond Collop for always being willing to help. For time so freely given. A million thank you's. Your expert insight was invaluable, *and all errors are my own.*

To my Badass Typewriter babes, Collette Kelly and Therese Beharrie. No words can express my gratitude for the love, support and friendship. You girls rock!

To Natasha Anders for the amazing mentoring. I am thankful to have shared this experience with you. It was an honour and a privilege to be mentored by you.

To Dani René for everything. There are simply no words to accurately say thank you for all you've done to help me put Love At Last in the hands of readers. Your unstinting support is appreciated more than I will ever be able to express fully. You are a rock star!

To Candy Royer for the fabulous job you did editing this book. It was a pleasure and an honour working with you. I look forward to our next project together. And Illuminate Author Services for the wonderful job proofreading. Thank you!

Thank you to my beta readers. Your feedback was invaluable and much appreciated. I look forward to working with you again soon. And to all the ROSA ladies for their unflagging support and generosity.

And finally, to you the reader, a deep and heartfelt thank you. Your support means more than I can ever express. I hope you came to love Adam and Willow as much as I do.

Much love,

Dorothy xx

ABOUT THE DOROTHY

A proud member of the Romance Writer's Organization of South Africa (ROSA), Dorothy Ewels developed a love of reading from early on. Her passion for the written word has spanned across decades until she finally put pen to paper and began her path as an indie author where reading and writing remain her first love.

Married, with one son and three fur babies, she lives in Cape Town, and while she loves travelling, she cannot see herself living anywhere else. When she's not weaving stories in her writing cave, she spends her time with family, friends, as well as enjoying crafting.

OTHER BOOKS BY DOROTHY

One Night Only – a shorty-short story

FIND DOROTHY ONLINE

WEBSITE

http://www.dorothyewels.co.za

FACEBOOK

https://www.facebook.com/dorothyewelsauthor

TWITTER

https://www.twitter.com/DorothyEwels

INSTAGRAM

https://www.instagram.com/dorothyewelswrites

AMAZON

https://www.amazon.com/author/dorothyewels

GOODREADS

https://www.goodreads.com/author/

show/18573939.Dorothy_Ewels

BOOKBUB

https://www.bookbub.com/profile/dorothy-ewels